D0399846

The French Impressionist

Rebecca Bischoff

Amberjack Publishing
New York, New York

Amberjack Publishing
228 Park Avenue S #89611
New York, NY 10003-1502
http://amberjackpublishing.com

This book is a work of fiction. Any references to real places are used fictitiously. Names, characters, fictitious places, and events are the products of the author's imagination, and any resemblance to actual persons, living or dead, places, or events is purely coincidental.

Publisher's Cataloging-in-Publication data
Names: Bischoff, Rebecca, author.
Title: The French impressionist / by Rebecca Bischoff.
Description: New York [New York] : Amberjack Publishing, 2016.
Identifiers: ISBN 978-1-944995-02-7 (pbk.) | 978-1-944995-03-4 (ebook) | PCN 2016939201
Subjects: LCSH Communicative disorders in adolescence--Fiction. | Runaways--Fiction. | Child abuse-- Fiction. | Mothers and daughters-- Fiction. | Nice (France)--Fiction. | BISAC YOUNG ADULT FICTION / Social Themes / Runaways | YOUNG ADULT FICTION / Social Themes / Disabilities & Special Needs | YOUNG ADULT FICTION / Social Themes / Physical & Emotional Abuse.
Classification: LCC PZ7.B5238 Fre 2016 | DDC [Fic]--dc23

Cover Design: Ashley Ruggirello of CardboardMonet.com
Roboto font used according to the terms of Apache License, Version 2.0.

Printed in the United States of America

One

I'm here because I lied. A lot.

I know it was wrong, but I don't care. I got away.

My world is no longer black and white. It's alive with color. Blues and greens have melted together into a perfect painting of sea and sky. I smell the sharp sweetness of citrus. It must be coming from the trees that line the street and quiver in the soft Mediterranean breeze. I breathe in the scents of hot sun on sand, salty ocean, and a puff of sugary, vanilla air exhaled from a nearby bakery. A tram whirs by and clangs its bell. A couple passes, so close that the woman's skirt brushes my bare legs with a whisper of touch. She murmurs in the unfamiliar cadences of a foreign language, leaving behind a cloud of gentle laughter. I start to laugh too. I take in my freedom like a drowning person gulps air. No matter how many more half-truths or total lies I have to tell, I'll do it.

I won't go back home.

Gripping the handle of my suitcase, I turn around. The sign above the shop door proclaims *Sylvie's Dream*, in English. Something inside me feels like it's warming, shifting, dissolving. My entire body wants to sag with relief, even though my pulse is now racing. *I made it. I'm actually here!*

The shop is on Rue Massena, part of Nice's old town. This part of the city feels old. When I look up from the street, the pink and gold buildings lean into one another and crowd around me like they're curious to find out who's invading their space. The paint on the walls is faded and peeling, and laundry hangs from lines that stretch between windows. Towels, jeans, and underwear wave in the breeze.

It's so different from anything I've ever known. I already love it. Now all I need to do is go in. At the thought, my heart flutters inside me like a bird flapping its wings, trying to escape from its cage.

Before I can lose my nerve, I step up to the door. They're both here. Even before I got out of the cab, I could see them through the speckled shop window. The woman is Sylvie. The man, Émile. They are the new family I chose.

Physically, they're as opposite as any two people can be. Sylvie is tall and thin, all dark hair and eyes, with skin a warm, melted chocolate brown. Émile is much shorter, no more than a few inches taller than I am. Nearly everything about him is light-colored. He has papery skin and white hair that make his indigo eyes jump out at you. When he stands beside Sylvie, he looks like a ghost.

I already know them. I already love them. But will they love me? Okay, back up a little. That comes later. For right here and now, what will they say? They didn't expect me until next Friday, but here I am, thanks to a timing glitch. I misread the dates of the real summer program here in Nice when I was creating my fake art camp to fool my mother. I'm not supposed to be here yet, but I had no choice.

Go, I tell myself, suddenly feeling the need to swallow, hard. *It's time.*

My entire body starts to tremble as I push through the strands of tiny brown seashells that form a tinkling curtain in the shop's doorway. The handle of my case catches onto something and I stumble, but recover quickly and plant a smile on my face.

"Um," I say, fumbling in my pocket for my carefully crafted note, but then Sylvie sees me and her face lights up like the summer sun.

"*Rosemary, oui? C'est toi!* It's you," she exclaims, before spewing a thousand more French-sounding syllables that I don't understand, as her brown arms encircle me and squeeze. She smells like lemons and coconut, and in my head I see long stretches of pale sand against a turquoise ocean. A vision of freedom. *My* freedom.

Sylvie releases me and before I can process anything, Émile is before me, his face level with mine. His eyes crinkle as he grins. He takes my hand and squeezes softly.

"*Bienvenue*," he murmurs. "Welcome."

"*Merci*," I whisper, and am horrified at how the word sounds as it leaves my lips, but no one seems to notice. Émile and Sylvie grin expectantly at me, so I finally take out my note.

Sylvie peers over her husband's shoulder to read as I set my case down and gaze around me, trying to pretend that I'm not terrified, that I'm not desperate for this to work.

Sylvie's artwork splashes color across the walls, like a paint factory explosion. There's a battered cooler in the corner with a hand-written sign offering bottles of water, Orangina, ice cream, and candy bars. Stuff is piled everywhere. Books, necklaces, pottery, a rack of brightly colored skirts. It's a place that holds the promise of hidden treasures for anyone who wants to look. Messy, but cozy. The tiny space extends soft arms that pull you into a warm hug, a lot like its owners. It's perfect.

They look up from the note.

"*Eh, bien*, you are early, but it's no matter," Sylvie says in slow, careful French. "I am sorry that you've lost your voice. We're so happy that you're here! Émile will take you to your room."

Émile takes my suitcase and gestures for me to follow him and I do, finally remembering to breathe. I suck in oxygen while we climb the narrow, wooden steps that lead up from the back of the shop. My new father says nothing. I'm sure it's out of pity for the fake illness that caused me to lose my voice. I hope.

We move into a cool, dark hallway and Émile opens a door for me. I step inside and gasp. I've seen a photo of the room, of course, on Sylvie's blog, but pictures never compare to reality. This room is warm and alive with color.

Émile smiles. "I hope you like your bedroom. It was our son's." With that, he places my suitcase onto the floor and turns to leave, before glancing back.

"You would like to rest?" he asks me, his eyebrows raised. His French is slow, too, even slower than Sylvie's. They are so kind. So patient. I want to say something, but can't make any words come out. Not a single sound. To cover my embarrassment, I kneel to tie my shoe, praying he hasn't noticed that it wasn't untied in the first place.

"Stay here as long as you like," Émile says with a shrug. "Or you may join us in the shop, if you prefer," he adds. "When you wish." And with that, he is gone.

It worked. It worked!

I look around. My room, my beautiful new room, has forests and oceans and mountains painted all over the walls. It has stars and planets on the ceiling. A mustard-colored rug spattered with paint sits on the floor. On the bed is a vivid quilt that's a kaleidoscope of colors. The room has a window that looks out over red-tiled roofs and palm trees. It even has a cat! Amber eyes glow up at me from the puff of grey fluff resting on the rug.

I was never allowed to have a pet. I stare at the pile of grey fur for a second, not sure what to do. Will it chase me from its territory? But the puffball simply closes its yellowy eyes and goes to sleep.

I turn back, close the blue-painted door, and stare at the knob. There's no lock. On this side or on the other side.

It's perfect.

A couple of tears spill down my face, but I swipe them away. My new life just started, and I'm going to live it. I'm going to head back down to the shop and get to know my new family.

But when I grasp the doorknob, I stop. I don't want to leave just yet. I turn to check out the room one more time, straining a little to see the murals as the light from the window changes from bright to dim. Outside, clouds cover the sun and a summer storm spatters rain onto the glass. I don't bother to turn on the light, though. I know this room well already. I walk along the walls, tracing the paintings with a gentle finger. The photo of this room on Sylvie's blog was what started it all. It's part of the reason that I'm here and why I chose Sylvie and Émile to be my new family.

The mural at the head of the bed is my favorite. A trail curves through a forest, then up the side of a steep canyon, where it angles back and forth in sharp switchbacks. Every so often, along the trail is a boy who carries a backpack and walking stick. The boy, lanky and brown like Sylvie, gradually grows taller. It's their son, Ansel, now gone. He painted himself somewhere on the trail each year for his birthday. The figure at the very top of the cliff is Ansel at eighteen, heading to Paris. He's smiling and pumping a fist into the air.

I kiss my fingers and touch them to the painted boy's tiny head. "Thank you, Ansel," I whisper. I couldn't be here if he weren't gone. "I promise I'll take care of the room for you."

A gleam of light glows on the wall a few feet away. I jerk my hand back in surprise. Painted on the other side of Ansel's cliff is a wide expanse of stormy sky over a dark ocean. Streaks of bright lightning cross the gloomy haze, but one line of lightning extends downward in a straight line, cutting through sky and cloud until it plunges into the ocean. I move closer until my nose is practically against the paint and stare. The straight line, of course, isn't painted lightning. It's a crack in the wall, one so deep that light from the next room shines through it. Then, before I can even begin to wonder, the crack disappears.

What just happened?

Two

Lie Number One: I traveled to the sunny coast of France to study art.

Truth: I don't even know how to hold a paintbrush.

I came here to escape. But they can't know that. At least, not yet.

Émile sits and reads. Cross-legged in a puffy, cherry-colored chair in the corner, he kind of reminds me of a white Persian cat curled up on its cushion. He glances up as I re-enter the shop, smiles and nods, then goes back to his reading. Sylvie dabs at a canvas in front of her. She, too, looks over and winks with warm, sparkling eyes. She says something I don't understand, but I nod, and she seems content with whatever my gesture meant and turns back to her work.

I've just arrived from another country. I still have a stale, peanut aftertaste on my tongue, along with the flavor of that odd stuff from a tin that was like a meat-jello salad served on the flight. We met in person mere minutes ago, and this is all my hosts do when I come downstairs after unpacking? Nod and smile and leave me alone?

I did the right thing. This is beyond perfect.

I love my new parents.

Grinning like a total goofball, I shuffle around shelves and check out their stuff. On Sylvie's blog, the photo of her shop blew me away. It was so cool. *So French.* In person, it's like I stepped into a travel brochure, where you'd read words like *quaint* or *picturesque* in the captions. I pick up a book with a pyramid on its cover, which was shoved next to a book in German that has a photo of a bunch of Huskies tied to a sled. Maybe I'll read. I am worn out by my journey, driving on fumes, fuel tank empty, but I don't want to miss this, my new life. I want to stay here and hang with my new family.

"*Égypte*," Émile says, pointing and jabbering at my book. I sit on a low bench by the wall and open it, trying to paint a knowing expression on my face, like I know what the heck he's saying. Looking down, I see that the words are in a different language I don't recognize, but luckily the pages consist mainly of large, vivid photographs of mummies. Dried up people. I can relate. I know what it's like to feel like a husk of a person. Shriveled and already dead.

When Émile says something else to me, I have to admit defeat, which I do by shrugging apologetically. I'd love to ask him a thousand questions, beginning with: *Did you know there's a giant crack in the bedroom wall, and I saw light glowing from behind it?* I can't find the words. I'm too tired to shuffle through French vocabulary files I've painstakingly shoved for so long into my foggy brain. I've been traveling for nearly twenty-four hours, after all. So when Émile returns the shrug and goes back to his book, I close mine. It's making me sleepy to sit and stare at pictures anyway. I'll make myself useful and grab a broom.

The seashell curtain over the front door tinkles and sways as a hand reaches to sweep it aside. Customers. Glancing up, I flick my long, dark braid back over my shoulder.

A middle-aged couple shuffles inside. The man and woman blink as their eyes adjust to the dimness. My brain does a quick calculation. Pasty, Northern European skin that fries under too much coastal sun. Shorts, sneakers, fanny packs. *Touristes,* I say in my head. It feels fantastic to think that word. I'm not one of those. I live here.

A sudden shivery feeling shoots its way up my spine. A teenage boy with hair the color of a pumpkin ambles into the shop at the heels of the older couple. My mouth dries up. I've never seen a guy my age this close before. Seriously. That's an honest statement. No boys allowed in my former life.

I wander closer to the boy while I sweep away imaginary dirt. I'm the only fifteen-year-old I know who has never been alone with a guy. Ever. Not even a friend. No mall, no parties, no dates. And here I am, free for the first time to actually check somebody out. I can't help staring. The boy has freckles scattered across his nose and cheeks, like flecks of cinnamon sprinkled onto cream.

The old-ish tourists shuffle over to Sylvie, who has

popped up from her perch in front of her canvas. I keep sweeping away, moving myself ever so slowly, and inching closer to the fascinating owner of the freckles and red hair. He glances up from a rack of used books and grins. I grin back and feel my face flush. From behind me in the shop, the man speaks to Sylvie in English, Texan twang flying out of his mouth.

So they're Americans, like me. That doesn't matter. I've been rehearsing this for a long time. I'll give an apologetic shrug and say, "No English," with a hint of an accent. Then I'll add a sweet, seductive smile. I'll be the mysterious French girl whose face will linger in the boy's mind after he leaves. I breathe in, lick my lips, stand up straight and get ready to flirt for the first time in my life.

"*Ah, Americains!*" Sylvie calls. She continues to chatter, motioning for me to come. I don't have to understand her exact words. I know what she wants. Without realizing it, I let go of the broom and it falls to the floor with a clatter. I pick it up, face burning scarlet, and lean it against the wall, trying to ignore the fact that the boy is chuckling. My plan is shredded. In two seconds flat, the seductive French girl has morphed into a tongue-tied terror. I get how neurotic this sounds, but I can't help it. When I have to speak to strangers, something inside me shrivels.

But there's nothing I can do to avoid this, so I shuffle forward a few feet until I'm closer to Sylvie and the American couple. The boy grins and pops his gum and he moves closer as well. I follow him with my eyes. His mouth is gorgeous. He has full, curving lips.

"Uh, hi," I whisper, swallowing hard.

"Are there public restrooms nearby?" the woman asks me in English. Redhead rolls his eyes and smiles more widely at me.

The next few seconds feel like a thousand years. I try to find a way to communicate "bathroom" without saying the actual word. I do this a lot. As usual, I can't think fast enough. The silence starts to feel funny. They're all looking at me. I swear I hear a clock ticking, even though there isn't one in the shop. Finally, *finally*, I figure it out. I point down the street in the general direction of a public bathroom a couple of blocks away. Luckily, I'd seen the sign as the cab drove me here.

"Um, no. That way," I say, feeling a rush of relief when the words don't sound strange.

"A bathroom? Rosemary, tell them to come with me!" Sylvie says in slow French that I can understand.

"*Oh, je parle français, Madame,*" the Mom interjects, spewing perfect, slippery French words that slide right off her tongue.

What? Why didn't you just do that in the first place, you hag?

There was no need, no need *at all* for me to go through that torture.

"Perfect!" Sylvie says, beaming. "Let's go." She drops her paintbrush, actually drops it right onto the floor, and motions for them to follow her, babbling something about dirty public toilets. Grinning, Émile rises from his red chair and follows the group up the stairs to their cheerful apartment complete with sanitized bathroom.

The boy stays. I start to sweat. I'm alone. With a

guy. I look away and pretend to keep working. *I was going to flirt with him? Who was I kidding?* Then I sneak another look. I can't help it. He throws a half-grin my direction and then starts to wander around the shop. His smile is mischievous, but kind of sweet at the same time. Something inside me immediately wants to see that look on his face again. To be the one who put it there. Butterflies do a little happy dance in my stomach and my heart rate accelerates. *Why shouldn't I flirt?* My best friend Jada does it without saying a word. *I don't have to talk, remember?*

Glancing around, I see a feather duster and grab it. I begin to flick invisible dirt from shelves as I slowly move in the boy's direction.

I twitch feathers over the surface of a display case and move to dust a box full of polished rocks. I'm getting closer. I take a deep breath and glance at him. He's looking at me. I smile. He smiles back.

I'm flirting!

And then, after I fake-clean a shelf of paperback books, I'm as close to him as I can be without jumping into his arms. I panic. Now what?

He's looking at me. Come on, Rosemary! Okay, I'll talk, but stick to speaking French.

"Nice is pretty, isn't it?" I blurt in slurred, barely recognizable French. The boy looks up in surprise, still holding a figurine he'd picked up.

"What?" he answers in English.

Blood floods my face so fast that my skin prickles. What's with the blushing? I've done it more times than

I can count in the last five minutes! I shrug, try to smile, and repeat myself more slowly.

"Sorry, I don't speak French," he answers, setting the figurine down and holding out his hand. "I'm Gavin. What's your name?"

I take his hand. It feels warm and dry. I hope he can't feel how sweaty my own hand is. I look into his eyes, and realize with a start how unusual they are up close. They're a dark, coffee brown, but the lashes are so pale they're nearly colorless. His strange eyes seem to look right through me.

"And you are . . .?" the boy prompts, with another flash of his grin.

Oh, yeah. My name.

I can't say my own name easily, so I made up a new one. And at this moment, looking into black coffee eyes that are strangely naked with no visible fringe of lashes, I cannot remember what my new name was supposed to be. My mind is a hollow space. Footsteps are already pounding down the staircase. I have to say a name, and quick.

"Didn't you hear me?" the boy asks. Does he sound annoyed? I don't think so, but I can't tell. He's still holding my hand. He edges closer. I can smell bubblegum on his breath.

I breathe in, then out. And I blurt my name. My *real* name.

"Rosemary," I say, practically shouting. And then I want to die. Remember that whole "no guys" thing? I'm also the only fifteen-year-old I know who can't say her own name correctly. I hate talking to strangers for a good reason.

"What?" Gavin asks, stepping back. I can't read his expression. The corners of his mouth are turned up a tiny bit. Is he mocking me? He looks at me. I look back. I cave. I torpedo myself away until I'm standing beside a shelf of glass bottles filled with multi-colored sand at the back of the shop. I pick one up and pretend to be working again. I can practically hear the sizzle as my face fries.

Sylvie and Émile return with Gavin's parents. They move about the shop, now old friends, discussing Italian food, museums, and public toilets.

Gavin saunters over to me. In a soft voice that only I can hear, he murmurs, "Nice to meet you . . . Rosemary." He makes my name sound strange, mimicking the way I spoke.

My mouth falls open and I whirl to face him, one hand raised and clutching a little glass bottle, like I'm about to smash it onto his orange head.

We stare. His eyes are alight with amusement, but soon his face changes. He grimaces and squeezes his eyes shut as he ducks his head and rubs the back of his neck. When his dark eyes find mine again, his expression is guarded.

"Look, that was . . . No, I didn't mean . . ." he says.

He doesn't get to finish, because the glass bottle I'm holding slips from my sweaty fingers and splinters into a million pieces on the floor, scattering pale orange and pink sand across the worn wood.

Glass crunches as I crouch down among the shards,

trying to ignore the babble of voices around me. I was supposed to have lost my voice! Why didn't I remember that? My eyes burn.

I blink, hard. Gavin is still here, hovering above me. I refuse to be weak. I will *not* let this get to me.

Someone hands me a dustpan and I automatically start piling the larger fragments of glass into it, then brush the sand into a pile. I'm rewarded by a sharp sting on my palm. I gasp and look down at the blood that wells from the slash in my hand. Colored sand sticks to my blood and clammy skin, forming a sparkling spiral pattern, like the Milky Way. For a second or two, I forget where I am. The tiny fragments of sand catch the light and twinkle like a thousand miniature stars. I'm holding a glittering galaxy in the palm of my hand.

Sylvie helps me to my feet and says something I don't catch as she leads me to the metal sink at the back of the shop.

The American family leaves after the woman says something like, "Oh, ah hope she's all raht," in her abominable southern accent.

My galaxy dissolves in a swirl of blood, sparkling sand, and water that gurgles down the drain.

Oh, I'm all right, lady, just a little humiliated. It happens every day. Every. Day.

And then I start to laugh.

I flirted for the first time, ever, and it ended in disaster. The hot guy was a total punk. It did look like he was trying to apologize, but it doesn't matter.

He never should have done what he did in the first

place.

I wince as Sylvie smears some clear ointment that smells like wintergreen gum onto my palm, but I keep smiling.

The guy left. I am still here. In my new life.

"*Ça va*," I whisper, as Émile peers over my shoulder to check out the damage. I remember my laryngitis this time. I remember to avoid English.

It's okay. I'm okay.

But only if I don't forget my plan. Only if I play my part well.

Three

When I wake up from my nap, I don't know where I am for a second. Blinking, grimacing at the taste in my mouth that makes me think I recently ate something long dead and putrid, I sit up and search for the source of the weird sound that woke me up. It's like the soft hum of an engine far away. Maybe it's a plane.

Or a cat.

He's staring at me from the foot of the bed and making the sound, which I realize is purring.

"Hi," I whisper.

He stares.

"I like it when you do that," I add, wincing only a little at the way the words come out.

He blinks. He yawns.

At least he doesn't make fun of me.

I look over at the wall, to where Ansel's painted storm swirls. The lightning I saw earlier is gone, so the light behind it is off. *I've got to ask about that! What's back there?*

Swinging my legs over the bed, I check my phone. I have just enough time to engage in a little art therapy before dinner. Once my stick-figure of the ginger boy with coffee eyes and a mocking grin is complete, I toss him into the metal trash can and set him on fire with the match I found on the windowsill.

It's a mini funeral pyre. Satisfying. The paper shrivels as orange flames eat Gavin from toes to torso to head. Acrid smoke hits my nose. He is ashes.

Au revoir, Pumpkin Head. You are gone.

"Good enough?" I ask the cat. I toss my cell to the bed and watch it slide off onto the floor. Fat Cat hops down from his spot on the quilt and stares at the screen with vague interest for a second, before he curls up and closes his eyes yet again. His fur is like a sooty winter sky. I like him, despite his complete lack of social skills.

I reach out a tentative hand and stroke his impossibly soft fur. He purrs again. I sit cross-legged on the floor next to my new friend. A funny, foreign-sounding police siren passes by outside. Fat Cat stands, stretches and stalks away, and I feel like I've been dismissed. I don't mind. I get up too, and open the blinds so I can stare out at my new world.

By now the summer storm has ended, and the late afternoon sun casts a lemony glow on the city around me. Between pastel squares across the street is a narrow space where I glimpse a blur of blue water beyond rooftops and the shadows of palm trees. Quaint. Picturesque.

Freedom.

I lean my head on the cool glass. I have a chance for a new life, a *real* one, as long as I remember that I can't talk. Flirting for the first time was a disaster. *But Gavin was just so . . . pretty. Yeah, that's it.* I grin to myself. So he was a jerk. But he was a pretty jerk. I'll give him that.

I already feel better. Guess I had to learn the hard way. I can't forget the name I picked for meeting new guys. It's May. One syllable. No long combination of sounds that are supposed to line up just right. Nothing to get tangled. No "R"s to screw up.

May. I like it.

And I can't wait to try it out on someone. But for now, I really need to use the bathroom, so I hope Mom—

It hits me so hard I stop breathing. She's not here. She's far, far away. And I can leave this room any time I want.

My door opens with a soft squeak. The hall is empty and smells like dust and a musky perfume. There are framed black and white photos all along the walls, shots of the lost Ansel. I hear soft sounds from the kitchen. Sylvie, laughing. Émile talking, pots clinking, water running. My heart pounds in my ears and my palms start to sweat, because I'm not used to being alone like this.

The same thing happened on the plane for a while, until I finally took Benadryl and fell asleep.

Down the hall, I stumble into the bathroom. Yeah, the one Sylvie decided she had to share with strangers. I splash water on my face and the cold shocks me out of panic mode and I start breathing again.

When I look up from the towel, I see red. The

wallpaper, the shower curtain, and the rug are covered in roosters. Blood red is the predominate color scheme. *Isn't that a kitchen thing?* I brush my teeth and attack my tangles with such vicious energy I lose half my long hair in the process. When I pick up a painted wooden rooster that for some reason has long, human-like legs attached with wire, someone knocks at the door and I jump, dropping the thing on my bare toes.

Out of habit, I bite my lip to lock the word I was thinking inside my head, until I remember a nanosecond later that I am free to let it out. So I do. Under my breath. And it comes out all wrong.

Sylvie calls something in her chirpy voice and moves off down the hall.

I sit on the edge of the tub and rub my sore toes, repeating the curse word until it comes out right. I only feel mildly better when it finally does.

I've heard of support groups for people who drink or do drugs. They always introduce themselves by first sharing their weakness. It's like, "Hi. My name is James, and I'm an alcoholic." Or, "My name is Alina, and I'm a drug addict."

My name is Rosemary, and I have a communication disorder. It has a name, too, but I can't even say it.

So there you have it.

Lie Number Two: I am normal.

Truth: I am not.

Sylvie's cat is waiting for me. I have to step over him to get back into the bedroom. He doesn't move.

My phone beeps like R2D2. It's a text from Zander. I

take a deep breath.

Play your part. You're not totally free. Not yet.

So I read the message with bleary eyes:

Doing ok, R?

Yup.

I yawn so wide I think my jaw is about to break.

My hand twinges as I type. That cut was deep. When I look down at my bandaged palm, I remember the tiny galaxy I saw there. If I were a real artist, I would draw or paint and try to recapture the feeling I had when I looked at the blood and sand on my skin and saw the Milky Way. But I'm not.

Zander texts back.

Haven't heard from U since that text from
the plane. Tell Mom all OK.
She's a bit worried.

Crap. Now I'm wide awake. Zan's the king of understatement. What he means is that Mom is about to have a Class A, Super-Sized, Medication-Necessary break down. I was supposed to call her when I arrived at the "Red Rock Youth Art Camp." The one she thinks I'm attending in Arizona.

But I was busy. After the flight to Paris, I got my luggage and then had the most terrifying trip of my life. Clutching step-by-step instructions I'd carefully typed to help me get from airport to train station to cab to Sylvie's shop, I ran away from my life. I knew I'd get lost. I knew I'd screw up. But I didn't.

"Help me out, Fat Cat," I say, looking over at my new roommate. The grey ball of fuzz who has now spread his considerable feline form across the single chair in the room opens one eye, blinks at me for a second, and closes that eye again. This cat is no help whatsoever. I flop back onto the bed and stare at my phone.

Lie Number Three: Zander is my friend.

Truth: Zander is Mom's boyfriend. He's not *my* friend.

I stretch stiff legs and yawn again. Yeah, Zander did a lot to convince Mom to let me go to "art camp." He helped me get a passport and apply for a summer program in Paris. He took me to the Apple store to find out about international phone usage and how to deal with that. All the while telling Mom how great Arizona would be for me.

So, he lied to Mom. And I lied to him. And I'm still lying to him.

I have to. Because he has no clue about my mother. He doesn't see what she's really like.

So, after I think for a second, I send an email. Just a "sorry I forgot to call, Sedona is beautiful, thanks for letting me go to camp, *blah blah blah*," message to make Mom happy.

Then I email Zander, "Paris is amazing, this will really help my art, I owe you, *blah blah blah*."

I hit *send*.

Lie Number Four: I am in Arizona, according to my mother. I am in Paris, according to Zander.

Truth: I am in Nice, that palm-treed, stuccoed, touristy town in the south of France. No one knows this but me. Well, and one other person. It's complicated.

Émile taps on the door as he calls my name.

"*Entrez*," I answer, with slurred, fuzzy syllables that are way too loud. I keep forgetting that I told everyone I lost my voice. Idiot.

Émile enters and sits down in the wooden chair by the door. He smiles, and I grin in response. It's so easy to like him.

"Ça va, Rosie? Your hand is okay?" he asks.

He called me Rosie. I like it.

I nod yes. I already feel comfortable with this ghostly man with his intense, dark blue eyes. I want to ask him about the strange glowing crack in the wall but I still can't find the right words. Then Émile says something that blows the thought out of my brain.

"The Americans," he says in escargot-paced French, giving me time to catch the words, "the ones we met in the shop? They are going to dine with us tonight. Sylvie has made new friends. Let's go."

Well, I *was* okay.

Four

Smells of the dinner that Émile has been cooking float through the open door. Émile is also an artist. Like his wife and son, he studied in Paris, but he doesn't work with paints and brushes. He works with pots, pans, and razor-sharp knives. I read about it on Sylvie's blog.

"Hungry?" Émile doesn't wait for an answer, but rises and wipes his hands on the smudged apron tied around his waist. "Seafood. I hope you'll like it." He smiles and gestures for me to go through the door first.

Gee. Thanks.

I fake cough and wince like my throat hurts. At least I won't forget my charade. We head down the hallway.

The kitchen smells like garlic, lemons, and fish. Seafood is *fruits de mer*, in French. Fruits of the sea. I find that vaguely disturbing. Also, I hate fish.

They're here. The Mom. The Dad. The Guy Who Insulted Me. When we get to the table, Émile gestures to

Gavin, indicating that he take the chair right next to me. And Gavin does, with this weird, almost bland expression. Is he embarrassed? I hope so.

We sit. It's awkward, trying to ignore the person next to me. I smell his aftershave, kind of smoky; hear him swallow when he takes a drink. I catch bright flashes of flame-colored hair in the corner of my eye every so often when he moves his head.

No one really eats much at first, because Sylvie and Émile have decided to play a kind of "get to know you" guessing game, in my honor. It's not too bad once we start. Émile, conscious of my infantile French skills and fake laryngitis, asks me questions, and all I have to do is nod or shake my head. Soon, everyone knows that I love Impressionism (ha!), *Harry Potter*, my favorite color is lavender, I've never been to France before, and that I'm from a tiny town called Twin Falls, Idaho, which means nothing to anyone in the room. Why would it? It's the armpit of the universe.

Then it's everyone else's turn. I finally start to eat, and catch names and details. The mom is Valerie, a French teacher, which explains her ease with the language. The dad is Phil, a biology teacher. Mercifully, when Sylvie or Émile talk too fast, Valerie translates for Phil and Gavin, so I can understand most of the conversation. Gavin's a wannabe surfer, avid gamer, and sci-fi fan who wants to design video games.

I find myself wishing I could make some kind of comment only he would hear about people who end up living in mom and dad's basement. Unfortunately, sarcastic comments are impossible for me. Of course, I'm great at making the most perfectly-timed, cutting remarks. In my head.

"How is your hand?" Valerie asks me without warning. I glance up, startled. All eyes turn to me. Showtime. I feel like an invisible curtain was raised, and I'm alone in the spotlight.

I shrug and whisper, "Okay." I smile apologetically, pat my neck, and mouth the words, "No voice."

"*Oh, la la*, I'd forgotten!" Sylvie says. "I'll make something for you." She hops to her feet and bustles to the stove.

For a few minutes, quiet chatter follows and everyone eats. I'm allowed to sit in silence. No one asks me any more questions because I can't speak. Why have I never thought of this before?

Sylvie brings me a steaming cup of hot lemonade with honey. I sip in grateful silence and eat fish with butter sauce that has salty, little, green things in it that look like tiny peas. At least it's not vomit-inducing. Neither is the salad with oily dressing, but I pass on some rubbery fried squid. The nervous stomach I'd had since I learned Gavin would be here settles down. Maybe I'm off the hook. The guy is apparently ignoring me as much as I'm trying to ignore him.

And then, right at the moment when I get too comfortable, Gavin stops stuffing his face and speaks.

"So, Rosemary," he drawls in his backwoods southern accent, "we haven't heard much from you. I wanna know your story. How did a girl from Idaho end up here?" He wipes his mouth with his napkin and turns to me. His face is expectant, his eyes kind of . . . waiting. He wants to know how I'll respond to him.

I might have imagined it. I swear I might have made it all up in my head, but when he said my name, I was sure I heard him exaggerate the "r" sound at the beginning, drawing it out so that it was way too long.

Maybe he felt bad about before, but apparently, he's over that.

I pause, taking time to swallow the mouthful of bread that's suddenly bone-dry in my throat. Then I pull out my cell phone. Mom always hates when I use it to talk for me, but she isn't here, is she?

Keeping my face neutral, I type the words:

Not your business. Go home, hillbilly.

I hold the screen so only Gavin can see it, make sure he reads the words, then delete them.

Before Gavin can reply, Valerie pipes up, "Why, what a good idea, using your phone to talk for you when you can't. I'd never have thought of it."

She smiles at me and I grin right back at her.

Whah, thank you, I say in a chirpy Southern voice inside my head.

Maybe she's not as annoying as I first thought. Mom would never agree with that opinion. In Mom's mind, using anything else to speak for you is a crutch. A weakness to overcome.

"Can I borrow your phone? I didn't get to answer,"

Gavin says. He holds his hand out but I shove my cell into my pocket.

Valerie answers for me. "Of course you can't, Gav! You haven't lost your voice. Well, what *is* her story?" she says.

"My name is Gavin, *Valerie,*" Pumpkin-head says. I witness the venom-filled glare he shoots at his mom. So does everyone else.

I take another quick sip of my lemonade as I watch the little family drama unfold. Phil mutters something soft but harsh-sounding to his son, while I'm frankly relieved the attention is off me. I didn't need to type those stupid words! Gavin will be gone for good after dinner. I shouldn't have let him get to me.

Suddenly, Gavin speaks, loud and clear. "Rosemary didn't give me much time to read, but I caught something about studying the French language," he says.

I turn to him, wary. He grins at me, and his eyes gleam with a hint of the same malice he'd aimed at his mother. He winks at me.

"And . . . French kissing."

I stare at him for a nanosecond, reading a challenge in his brown eyes and amusement all over his face. His full lips twist into a smile. And without thinking, I dump my hot lemonade onto his lap.

He leaps up and swears while everyone else moves at the same time, so there's a sudden mini-explosion of people in the tiny, blue-tiled kitchen. Somehow I extricate myself from the group and reach the hallway outside the apartment. I lean on the closed door and listen to the raised voices inside. I'm breathing like I ran a marathon.

Did I just throw a hot drink onto a guy's lap and then bail? I blink, digesting this bit of information. *I did.*

I am so embarrassed.

And then I see what's in front of me. Walking along the hallway is a tiny, shriveled woman who shuffles by in a housecoat and dirty slippers. She stares at me with a suspicious gaze, like I'm going to try to grab the crumpled paper bag she holds clutched in her wrinkled hands.

I stare back.

Her eyes narrow. Finally, she whips her head around to face forward and heads up the nearby staircase. I glimpse bulging, blue veins on her skinny legs as she ascends and hear voices at my back, growing louder.

They're coming out.

Telling myself I'm only being polite, because I don't want to cause the poor Southerners any more discomfort, I inch my way down the hall and creep up the stairs to avoid any more unpleasant interactions. Luckily, the old lady is gone.

The fixture that lights the upper hallway goes on automatically when I reach the top step. There's a door to my left marked with the number 64, and a plastic potted palm at my right, so close I brush against its dusty fronds. There's one more door at the end of the long, narrow hall, but it's not marked.

More voices from the hall below chase me farther away so I head to the unmarked door. I keep telling myself I'm not running away from anything. I'm just sparing the feelings of others.

Rusted metal forms a tiny balcony that doesn't look

very sturdy, and narrow spiral stairs wind upward along the outer wall of the building. *My mother would have a heart attack at the thought of me climbing this rickety monstrosity.* The thought spurs me onward.

At the top, the stairs open up onto a flat roof that's been turned into a garden. Trees in huge pots line one side of the rooftop. Their leaves shiver in the soft blowing air. The space before me is covered with low wooden boxes that hold rose bushes, tons of flowers, or the spiky leaves of onions and feathery tops of carrots. One box holds wiry tendrils that spill out all over the place. I smell the perfume of the blossoms and the clean, earthy scent of wet soil.

I sit and look up at the rain-washed sky that glows as the sun sinks low. Then I lie down on the flat roof, actually *lie down* right on top of dirt and leaves and cigarette butts. And I smile like an idiot up at the blushing sky. This is what it's like to truly be alone. Everything inside me feels new. Polished. Shining. I can almost forget my latest humiliation.

And in the space of one tiny heartbeat, I know that I can't. Not really. I sit up and pick leaves from my hair.

It's always going to be like this. How can I forget? It's like there's this room full of people, all talking and laughing and having a great time and I'm watching through a wall of glass, wanting to join them.

The sun goes down as I explore every inch, pick a hard green apricot, smell the roses, drop petals from the roof, and finally decide that I've wasted enough time.

Downstairs, I listen at Sylvie's door to make sure

the Americans are gone. They are. I pause with my hand on the knob and try to gather some courage. I hear my therapist's voice in my mind. "Find your feet, Rosemary. Breathe." It sounds so stupid, but sometimes it works. Thinking about my feet is supposed to make me forget whatever's bothering me. It's also a symbol for stepping forward and moving on from the crap that happened. Then I just breathe. Out with the bad air. In with the good air.

I find my feet. I breathe. And I talk in my head.

Goodbye, Gavin. Y'all don't come back now, y'hear?

Sylvie meets me inside and enfolds me in a warm embrace. I hug her back, gratified and kind of shocked that she's showing such affection to a stranger. To an awkward girl who behaved like a toddler. My hopes heave themselves back off of the floor inside me.

When Sylvie releases me, she says nothing. Émile asks me if I'm still hungry, offers dessert, and that's all. For a second, he looks at me like there's something he wants to say, but he doesn't. So I sit and eat chocolate cake with fresh raspberries, and I feel dumb. Lame for running off the way I did. I make myself a promise. This is the last time I run away from anything.

New home.

New family.

New Rosemary.

Five

Truth: Jada is my best friend. Yes, she was chosen for me, but I love her. She's the real deal. This is no lie.

"Rosemary! How's Paris?" Jada asks, squealing with glee. I can tell she's turned up the volume on her laptop so I can hear her loud and clear. Even so, the synthesized voice Jada uses is almost drowned out by her very real giggles. Her voice is so loud I have to hold my cell away from my ear. Jada can laugh while she's talking but still have all her words come out steady and clear. She's got talent. Well that, and super-powered communication software that speaks for her.

Jada's the only other person on the planet who knows I'm not in Paris. But she doesn't know everything. I'm going to puke. I hate lying to my best friend. But I have to.

"Paris is amazing, J.," I tell her, feeling my "fruits of the sea" swimming around in my gut while I play along with Jada's little joke. "The Eiffel tower is way tall."

Jada snorts. She only does this when she's laughing really hard. She thinks she's in on everything. She thinks we just pulled one over big time on both my Mom and Zander. She doesn't know I'm pulling one over on her as well.

"Tall palm trees, too," she finally manages to say.

My laugh is forced. I hope she doesn't notice.

Jada's at school, during free period. This is when we decided we'd call each other. I say something lame about how pretty the ocean is and switch topics in less than a heartbeat so she can't ask anything else. I describe Gavin (coffee, pumpkins, and the heart of a viper). I tell her about the broken bottle and my cut hand, and then the disastrous dinner.

It feels so good to have someone to share this with. While I talk, the tension melts off me like wax dripping from a candle. My words come out all garbled but Jada understands me better than anyone. Maybe it's because I know my bestie understands me, so I relax and words come easier. Jada not only gets what I say, but how I feel, too. She knows how it is to be the freak of the day.

When I get to the part where I dumped my hot lemonade onto Gavin's lap, Jada laughs so hard she gets hiccups. This cracks me up so we just sit there, giggling over the phone for like, forever.

Finally Jada regains control. "I forgot the new name. What was it?"

"Well," I answer, hesitating. "It's May, but maybe I need a better one. One I can't forget."

"Come on!" is Jada's response. I can tell she's about

to say more because of the way she breathes. It takes her effort to talk, too. Way more effort than me, since she can't even control her laptop with her hands. She has to hit a switch with the side of her head to move the mouse and make it click on the words she wants. This is actually an advantage on my part, because I always have time to think of what I'm going to say next when Jada is getting ready to answer.

"Jerubadissah," she finally says.

"That's so mean!" I answer, but I'm laughing. I know Jada said it on purpose. She's teasing me.

"Gotta go. New name, okay?" Jada says.

"Okay."

"Bring it, sister," Jada says. Then she's gone. "Bring it" is her way of telling me to be strong. To be brave. To stand up for myself.

I stare at the photo of Jada that glows from my cell phone screen. Jada's mom always calls us the "Opposite Twins." As far as physical appearance, we're kind of like Sylvie and Émile. Jada's eyes are green and her short, spiky hair is ash blonde. My eyes are brown, and my dark hair is heavy and long. But on the inside, they all say we're like twins. Same soul, different bodies.

Whatever.

It's true that Jada and I are very different in a physical sense, even down to the things that don't work correctly. Jada's body doesn't do what she tells it to do. Her legs and arms don't obey the signals from her brain. Her mouth doesn't either. As for me, well, it's only my tongue that's broken. That's all. But my words are so tangled that sometimes I wish I could use something to do the talking for me, like Jada. But Mom says no. She says I don't need it. It would be a crutch.

Exhaustion is dragging my eyelids closed. Jada's mom is wrong about us. My bestie and I are as different inside as we are on the outside. Jada never lets anyone make fun of her. She always has a comeback. Not me. I stand there with my heart in my throat, like a wounded animal. I only have good comebacks inside my head.

I snuggle down into my comfy bed and listen to the radio on my cell phone, letting the musical, nasally tones of the French language soothe me to sleep. Like I often do, I pretend that it's my voice I hear, forming perfect, fluid, silvery words that drop from my lips without any effort. Without even a thought.

Rolling over onto my side, I stare blankly at Ansel's murals, which are barely visible. *What would it be like to be normal? To have a brain that wasn't wired to make me sound like an idiot every time I opened my mouth?*

A new song comes on. I catch some of it, "They killed Spiderman! Nobody knows who did it. Maybe it was the Mafia." I start to laugh. It's cool that I can understand words in a different language. I so totally can't say them, though.

Anyone who knows me would think I was insane to try to learn another language, when I can't even speak my own.

I would have thought that too, if it weren't for Jada.

She forced me to take French with her last year.

"Everyone else will sound just as bad," she insisted.

And the most amazing thing happened.

She was right.

That day, the plan started to form in my brain. Jada came up with part of it. I owe her. Big time.

My bed is so soft. I yawn and stretch out. I don't remember falling asleep. Usually the nightmares wake me, but I must have been too exhausted to dream. This time, noise tears me from my sleep. The bedside clock tells me it's three in the morning.

I hear sounds. A soft thump, then sliding noises, like something being moved. *Thump . . . bump . . . clump.* The noises come from the other side of my wall, the painted wall where light shone through a crack. I'd finally managed to ask Sylvie about it after dinner. I couldn't figure out how to talk about the crack in the wall that glowed because a light shone behind it, but I asked who lived next door to us. And the answer was, "No one has lived there for fifty years." There's nothing but an empty apartment behind the painted wall in this room.

My lungs ache from the strain of holding my breath as I sit up in bed, listening. Then, softly, above my head, I hear more noises. They're moving upward, to the next floor. More soft bumps, a thud, and a voice murmuring words. A door slamming shut. Finally, silence.

Fuzzy-socked feet make no sound on the wooden floor. Sylvie's cat grumbles at me as I shove him aside with my foot. I've decided to call him "Fat Cat," since I can't understand, much less say, the name Sylvie told me. Stepping over him, I open my bedroom door. My heart does a little cartwheel. *I'm opening my door at night, leaving my room! There's no lock on the other side.*

The hallway is dark. Sylvie and Émile must be asleep. Émile's thunder-rumble snores fill the air.

The front door opens with a soft squeak and the outer hall light automatically clicks on. I ease the apartment door closed and tiptoe down the hall and up the stairs, feeling my pulse quicken. I don't know what I expect to find. Maybe a light behind one of the apartment doors upstairs? What would that tell me? I'm not sure, but I do know one thing, as I creep along in my worn-out pjs and green fuzzy socks at three in the morning, I am happy. I like my alone-ness. I like knowing that I can go wherever I choose. I don't have to ask anyone. I take a deep breath. Even the air is different when you're by yourself. No one else is there to steal your oxygen.

The old wooden stairs creak under my feet. I pause, trying to tread lightly. Is this nothing more than curiosity, or am I doing this simply because I can? Either way, I'm probably being stupid. All I can say in my defense is that I just want to *know*. I want to know what those sounds were that I heard coming from an apartment that's supposed to have been empty for half a century.

As I get closer to the top of the stairs, I hunch over and creep upward, hugging the wall until I'm almost at the top step. I don't want the automatic lights to turn on.

Skylights let in enough faint, watery moonlight for me to view my surroundings. To the right is the plastic palm tree, part of a fake jungle made of ugly pretend plants. To my left is apartment number 64, obviously the home of that old lady I saw earlier. The sounds are coming from behind that door. I stumble backward down several steps and crouch against the wall, holding my breath.

A door opens and light, shuffling footsteps creep across the hall in the darkness. The automatic light in the upper hallway clicks on. I move up a few steps but keep far enough away that I know I won't be seen. I hear what sounds like something heavy being moved. A voice grunts with the effort. Finally, I hear the same slow footsteps cross the hall again. A door closes.

Hardly daring to breathe, I inch upward. The little jungle to my right looks different, like stuff has been rearranged, and then behind dusty palm fronds, I see it. A door. I should have known. There's another apartment on this side of the building, behind the fake foliage, and it must connect to the so-called empty apartment below. Why did someone go inside? And why is the apartment door up here hidden behind a bunch of plastic plants?

I lower myself down to sit on the stairs. This shouldn't matter to me. It's none of my business. *But*, I think, picking lint from my socks, *somebody is hiding a secret. I mean, who moves heavy things around like that in the middle of the night?*

The automatic light from the hallway above clicks off and I'm left in the dark. It's kind of creepy. I shiver as my curiosity drains away. Sometimes being alone is scary.

I shrug as I stand, ready to give up the quest. At that moment I discover my mistake. The automatic hall light above clicks back on and I freeze. Only a few feet above my head, I hear shuffling noises from behind the door on the left. Whoever is in there saw that the hall light went back on! Trembling, I watch as a shadow appears behind the frosted glass square in that apartment door. It looms up, distorted and strange, like something out of a horror movie.

So, for the second time today, I run for it. Halfway down the steps, my feet, encased in their slippery socks, fly out from under me and I fall, hard, right on my backside. I bounce down the last few steps on my tailbone. I can barely walk but make it back to Sylvie and Émile's apartment hunched over in a kind of half-crouch, rubbing my sore butt.

Émile is still snoring. I quiver, hovering just inside the apartment with the door cracked open, holding my breath, listening for noise in the hall. After a few heartbeats, I hear it, shuffling footsteps that head down the stairs.

Stupid automatic lights.

The one above Émile and Sylvie's door flickered on when I hobbled back in here. That person will see the light and know that someone from this apartment was spying! *What should I do?* I listen, frozen in place, as the footsteps shuffle closer. I'm about to slam and lock Sylvie and Émile's door, but then I hear a woman's voice speaking French.

"*Occupe-toi de tes oignons,*" the voice calls out in a gravelly half-whisper. Mind your own business.

Then shuffling footsteps go back up the steps. I hear a door thump closed from the floor above me.

Laughter bubbles up and I have to clamp my hand over my mouth to keep from making noise. *That was it? That's what I waited for with sweaty palms and shaking legs?*

I ease the apartment door closed and lock it, still giggling. Then I rummage around in the fridge. I thought I'd seen a Coke in there, and I was right. Mom never allows soda. Sugar and caffeine are poisoning America's youth, along with preservatives like BHT. I grab the can and pop the lid. It tastes better than I could have imagined.

Mind my own business? I don't think so. I want to know what that old lady is doing inside the empty apartment. And I can if I want to. I'm free.

I gulp more soda and grin.

Six

The tiny alleyway that twists in front of me is how I always imagined the streets of old Europe to be. It's shoulder-wide and paved with uneven cobblestones. The walls on either side are crying. Dew trickles down them like tears trailing down worn cheeks. Every so often, I find tiny alcoves at eye level. They hold miniature statues of saints, with faded plaques bearing their names. There's one a few feet away from me, a sorrowful Virgin Mary. A woman brushes past me, mumbling to herself. Dressed in heels and a short skirt, she comes to a stumbling stop, kisses her fingers and touches Mary's face, and walks away without looking back.

There are no street signs here. I don't want to get lost, but I can't stop myself from moving. I'm in a strange city where nobody gives me a second look. I'm in a foreign country and nobody cares. I like it. Sylvie and Émile didn't bat an eye when I wrote them a note that read, "I want to go for a walk." They shrugged and smiled.

Now my heart's pounding and it won't slow down. It's like I'm high on the feeling of being by myself.

I pass a tiny courtyard hidden behind an iron gate. Inside, an old woman dumps towels into a rusty washing machine precariously perched against the wall. A narrow doorway in the side of the next building opens onto a steep, winding stair. The stairway smells liked cooked onions. At the top is a bright green door with a handwritten sign that proclaims: "Church of the Seven Wizards." I try the door. It's locked, of course, but then I see the key hanging on a nail high up in the corner. It fits in the lock and the door opens onto a dingy room that holds a few folding chairs placed around a card table. Bare shelves line one wall and cigarette butts litter the floor. The wizards aren't home.

I find my way back to the shop. Before I go in, I pass a little girl with stringy blonde hair and a runny nose playing on her front steps. She offers me a cookie. I take it. I eat it. Mom would remind me about the germs. And the sugar. And the gluten.

Dear Rosemary,

I miss you so much! I feel lost without you. It's Tuesday, and we're supposed to go to Kiwi Loco and have our yogurt together like we always do. I couldn't even stand to drive by the place! I worry that whoever feeds you at this camp won't stick to your dietary guidelines. Please make sure they follow my directions exactly. Write back!

Mom

Dear Mom,

Art Camp is awesome! They feed us well. This week we get French cuisine. I'm avoiding sugar, soy, and dairy, I promise. The cook knows I'm doing gluten-free, too, so no worries! I'm learning how to throw clay to make pottery. Soon I start painting class. Here's a picture of last night's sunset. It's gorgeous here.

Love ya,
Rosemary

There are millions of free online photos, if you know where to find them. My mother is completely helpless when it comes to technology, too. She can barely work her smartphone. Zan and I always have to help her. It's a huge advantage for me. This was almost too easy.

"Welcome back," Émile greets me as I reenter the shop, finishing my cookie. I nod at him and wipe the crumbs off my fingers.

We won't start painting lessons today. Sylvie is working on mosaics for an upcoming show. I can watch and learn if I want. I declined. I chose to spend my day here, in the shop. Mornings are always slow, I'm told. So far it's true. No one but us is here right now, though I'd be okay with customers. Really. There's only one person I don't want to see. After last night, I'm sure he's the very last human being I'll ever see again. Score.

Sitting behind the cash register in the sleepy shop on a languid summer morning, I pull out my cell and look at the day planner app as Émile yawns and leafs through a cook book. My life was always scheduled for me, and every moment of each carefully planned day is on my phone. The phone is supposed to beep at me when it's time to move on to the next scheduled activity. I turned off the alarms when I got on the plane. When I look at my schedule now, I see I didn't quite go far enough. Munching on an ice cream sandwich Émile handed me from the cooler in the corner, I delete each item, one by one.

6:45 a.m. My door is unlocked. I shower and dress in the clothing laid out for me.

7:30 a.m. Breakfast. (Gluten-free cereal, soy milk. Fresh fruit. Special vitamin formulated for children with communication disorders).

8:05 a.m. Drive to school.

8:27 a.m. Arrive at school. Mom walks me to class; goes to her office down the hall.

8:35 to 11:15 a.m. Morning classes. I check in with Mom in between classes, drop off my homework and exchange books. That's why I don't have a locker. Mom told the principal it was unnecessary.

11:15 to 11:45 a.m. Lunch with Mom. We eat our sack lunches in her office. It's better than eating in the cafeteria. I can't stand having everyone stare at us. Especially on Monday, or as Mom calls it, "Matching Shirt Monday."

11:45 a.m. to 3:15 p.m. Afternoon classes. I check in with Mom and exchange books, like I do in the morning.

3:25 p.m. Mom drives me home.

After school? Homework. Mom hovers, helps. Speech therapy sessions. Mom observes, takes notes. Speech practice. With Mom. Free time. With Mom. Sometimes Jada comes over. Her parents drop her off, and we'll chat, watch G rated, mother-approved movies or play G-rated, mother-approved video games.

With Mom.

Delete, delete, delete! I love the sound my phone makes each time I erase part of my old life. To my ears, it's a little bell ringing in triumph. Finally, there's only one item left.

9:30 p.m. Bed time. Mom says goodnight and locks my door from the outside. I can hear the grating, metallic *click* in my mind, clearly, as if it's happening right now. Mom's the only one who has a key.

The phrase, "Delete selected item?" blinks at me from my cell. I hit "Yes," and the screen of my phone glows a gorgeous, empty, electronic blue. Now each activity is gone. If it's not on my phone, it doesn't exist. Every day is now a blank canvas, and I'm the one who gets to fill it, any way I choose.

Émile yawns again and I do too. A sleepy morning, with nowhere to be, nothing particular to do, is a luxury I've never had before.

Later, I snooze the afternoon away. Sylvie laughed and said something about jet lag when I nearly fell asleep in my soup, and I allowed myself the freedom of a long, uninterrupted nap.

Did I mention that I like it here?

After dinner, all three of us watch some weird movie I half understand. My new French parents are content, smiling. I cuddle Fat Cat and text Mom. It's only morning for her, and supposed to be for me, too. I tell her I'm going to learn how to draw the human form. Oops. Then I have to spend about fifteen minutes promising that I won't be sitting before a bunch of live, nude models.

Once I'm in bed, the big cat's low purr lulls me to sleep. Soon I'm dreaming. My mother doesn't even like to doodle, but in the dream, I'm watching her paint the portrait of a girl. The girl on the canvas looks back at me from over her shoulder. Her hair is long, winds around her neck and is tight around her face, covering her mouth. I start to breathe hard and I try to ask my mother fix the painting, try to get the girl's hair off her face, off her mouth so she can breathe, so she can talk, but Mom won't answer me.

I can't breathe. I sit up gasping for air. I don't know where I am. I'm terrified. Suddenly, a sharp line of light glows on the wall beside me. I go completely still, except for the pounding of my heart that gradually slows.

Breath comes back to my body as the dream dissolves, and I understand at once that it was just another one of my nightmares. It was weird, though. Usually, I dream about a set of odd images that I can't explain. An old-fashioned dress with puffy sleeves and a torn hem. A sagging plaid couch with springs that poke through the fabric. A filthy teddy bear missing an eye. Canned peaches. Peanut butter on crackers. Always, those images fill me with a sense of quivering dread bordering on sheer panic. Yeah, I know. Peaches? Peanut butter? I can't figure it out either, but I've never been able to even look at that stuff.

I turn on the bedside lamp with a shaky hand, and check out the wall where the light glows through the crack. That's not any old crack on my wall. It's too tall. Too straight. There's a door.

I fling away fading nightmares and plan an attack. Padding across the cool blue-tiled kitchen floor, I mentally thank Émile for being such a good cook. Aside from the fact that his meals rock, he has an awesome set of cutlery. In no time I'm back in the bedroom wielding a wicked-looking knife.

Using only the dim reading lamp to guide me, I push against the glowing line of light. Under the pressure of my hand, the wall gives a little. *Is the crack a tiny bit wider?* I think it is. I was right. There was once a door in this wall. It was painted over. *Where was the knob?* My fingers find it, a slight bulge where a hole was covered with plaster.

I work the knife into the bulge and chip away the paint. Yellowish plaster flakes and falls onto the floor. The knife plunges a few inches into the hole I've created, scrapes against something. Using a flashlight, I can see dusty metal rods but not much else. I try to move them with my fingers. Nothing. I chip away more plaster. Still nothing moves. I'm tired and sweaty and annoyed, but then I move the knife sideways and hear a scrape and a click. The wall in front of me groans and moves away.

Flecks of paint fall into my hair. A rush of hot, stale air hits my face while at the same time my brain registers soft crackling sounds. I blink in surprise and look up. Oh, no. What was I thinking? When the door in my wall opened, the paint that covered the minute space between door and frame cracked and crumbled away. Long parallel lines extend from the floor to about a foot from the ceiling, where a horizontal line joins them. I've ruined part of Ansel's painting and left telltale signs on the wall of my midnight misdeeds.

How do I explain this? Before I can figure out what to do, Fat Cat jumps down from the bed and zooms into the dark space of the newly-opened doorway.

"Fat Cat, come back!" I stage-whisper.

I hear his low "mrrrrrr," and jangling collar bells, sounding muffled and far away. *Stupid cat.* Now I have to find him before I can do anything to fix my wall. I grab my cell, figuring I can use it as a flashlight, and step into the stale air behind the door in my wall.

Seven

The first thing that hits me is the smell of old dust. The place reeks like a museum. The weak light from my cell sends out a short beam that ends only inches in front of my face. Beyond that is nothing but a wall of darkness, but Fat Cat's bells tinkle from somewhere ahead. I move the light and find myself in a narrow hall. There's a small square opening a few feet away.

"Fat Cat!" I hiss. Darn him! That dwarf-sized door is kind of creepy. It's so low I have to crouch down to go through. Fat Cat finally answers, sounding even farther away than before. I take a deep breath and crawl through the tiny opening, and then I have to edge around a big, solid-looking thing covered with a dusty cloth. My light beam shows me a large open area, and lots of weird shapes, and I almost scream, because eyes are looking at me. Heart in my throat, I realize it's a painting.

When I look around, I can't believe what I'm seeing.

Paintings are everywhere; they're on the walls, on tables, on chairs, on the floor. This single room looks like it has more artwork than a gallery. I gawk at everything in full shock mode. The cloth-covered furniture crowds around me like lumpy ghosts trying to edge closer, and everywhere I aim the glow from my cell phone I see paintings, books, and papers piled in random jumbles.

Ancient wallpaper is peeling away from the wall in spots. Big flaps hang down and brush the floor. Moving the light beam, I jump when it reflects back into my eyes. The light was bouncing off a tall mirror with a gold frame. My footsteps are muffled by a thick carpet that feels gritty under my bare feet.

I should be scared. I should be in a hurry to find Fat Cat and get out. But I can't help another feeling that creeps over me. It's a funny mix of excitement and defiance. I'm breaking and entering. Well, something like that. My mother would definitely not approve.

Tearing sounds come from another room and I jump a mile out of my skin. Then, I hear Fat Cat's growly voice, and I hurry to wind through and around strange objects in the dark, because I know that Fat Cat likes to sharpen his claws. There's probably a lot of stuff in here that he'd shred if he got the chance.

I find him in the next room. Instead of an art gallery, this long rectangular space is a menagerie. In the dim glow of my flashlight, a stuffed Mickey Mouse and a toy pig next to him stare at me in wide-eyed surprise. Both look old-fashioned, and the threadbare toys are covered with dust, like everything else in here. A rusted birdcage hangs from the ceiling, and one shelf is jammed with stuffed birds, from tiny swallows to a massive owl with outspread wings. Fat Cat is trying to shred a dead ostrich bigger than I am. I grab the cat by his collar and pull him off while a few moldy feathers float to the floor.

While I back away, gripping the collar of my solid feline friend, my thoughts are muddy with confusion. Hundreds of paintings, furniture, and dead birds? And all in an empty apartment that nobody has lived in for decades. Why? Why didn't the people who left take this stuff with them? Then I hear a sound. Water gurgles through pipes above my head. Someone flushed a toilet upstairs. I have to get out of here, fast. What if that person were to come down here and find me?

Still dragging Fat Cat, I try to get back out to the room where I'd come in, but it's so dark. There's so much furniture crowded around me, and so much stuff piled on top of other stuff that I get confused. I go through a doorway and my phone light shows me a prehistoric-looking stone sink and a table with tall chairs around it. I back out and try again. I have to move all hunched over so I can hold onto the cat's collar. When I find another doorway, my foot hits something hard, and before I can stop myself, I yelp. I've found a stairway. This is the way to the next floor. I back up again, and as I do, I stumble over something and hear the sound of heavy things sliding to the floor, one by one: thump, thump, thump.

It takes my heart a minute to stop trying to escape from my chest. I stand, completely still, listening, trying to breathe without a sound. So far, I don't hear anything from upstairs.

But the moment I move, a door opens somewhere above my head, and a man's voice calls out in English, "Who's there?"

Fat Cat, you're on your own.

I let go of his collar and he zips away. I straighten and aim my light around the room, until finally I find what must be the right doorway, and shoot through it. Wrong again.

It's a bedroom, with a huge bed that's so high I'd need a ladder to climb onto it, four big wooden posts, torn curtains, and I'm out of time. Footsteps thud down the stairs. I'm trapped.

What do I do? I have to hide! Panic sets in and I whirl around like I'm trying to make myself dizzy, and my cell phone glow reveals brief glimpses of the round mirror of a dressing table and oval portraits on the wall. My panicked brain registers a massive wooden cupboard that stands against one wall, so I run and yank on the doors. They don't budge. By now the heavy footsteps are at the bottom of the stairs. The gruff voice is now mumbling inside the apartment.

I remember to switch off my phone the very moment I notice a large woven screen in the corner. I stumble over to it in total darkness, reach it and swing myself around to the other side, and a light turns on in the next room.

Hard objects dig into my back as I try to shrink against the wall. Fumbling around, I feel tall wooden frames behind me. More paintings are stacked behind the screen. Some are as tall as I am. Perfect! I worm myself into the space behind them, leaning them back against the wall so they form a kind of tent over my head. Then I crouch down and wait, breathing in dust and trying not to make any sound.

The man is moving around, switching on lights, calling again and again, "Who's there?" and pushing things around so he can look into all the rooms. He sounds big and he speaks with a British accent. This scares me even more for some reason.

The bedroom light goes on. The guy checks the big cupboard and rattles the locked doors. He moves toward the bed, and I hear the torn curtains being pushed aside. He sneezes and mutters something about how filthy the place is. I hold one hand over my mouth and nose and try not to breathe, but I'm sure he'll hear the sound of my heart, banging on my ribcage like a prisoner who wants to get out.

He moves closer. The screen rattles as it's pushed aside, and my insides are flooded with ice. The tall paintings that protect me shudder. He's moving them away from the wall, one by one. I'm frozen with terror. Every self-defense class Mom made me take did not prepare me for this. The guy's voice seems to come from ten stories above my head. Trying to stay calm, I clench my phone in my fist and get ready to strike. If I can hit him in the face, maybe I'll have a few seconds to get away.

The final painting shifts and begins to move. I tense, ready to spring forward and strike, but a sound comes from another room. Jangling bells! The ones on Fat Cat's collar.

The man hears them too, because the paintings suddenly drop back into place, hitting the wall above my head as they fall like dominoes. I gasp in shock and pray the guy didn't hear me.

Luckily, he must not have. His rapid footsteps thunder away and the bedroom plunges into darkness. I strain to listen as the man continues to search, pushing things to the floor, opening and closing cabinets, doors, stomping, muttering to himself, calling out, but Fat Cat's bells are now silent. Finally, the glow from the other rooms go out as he switches lights off, one by one.

Footsteps pound back up the stairs. I wait, my legs scrunched up under me, my feet numb. At last, a door slams above. The dead, dusty silence that falls once more in the ancient apartment is the most beautiful thing I've ever heard. I don't want to move. I sit, hugging my cell phone and mentally thanking Fat Cat. I count to one hundred. Then I count to three hundred. When I get to four hundred forty-nine, I hear Jada's laugh in my head, and know she would think I was a complete loser for cowering in here for so long. I finally move.

My numb legs don't work at first, so I crawl on the gritty carpet in the dark, and make it back to the bedroom door. By this time, the moon is shining softly through one of the windows in the room I call the menagerie. It lights the other doorways and I find the one I missed. Able to stand on tingling legs, I inch my way through the crowded rooms, back through the dwarf-door to the narrow passageway and the door in my bedroom wall.

Fat Cat is on my bed, purring.

"Stupid cat," I hiss at him, after I've grabbed him and hugged his solid body to me. He *did* save me. What would have happened if the man hadn't heard the bells? Fat Cat starts to purr. I collapse onto the bed. My nose if full of old dust and moldy smells, my feet, hands, and knees are filthy, and there are new holes and cracks on my bedroom wall that I'll somehow have to hide.

In the bathroom, I wash away the evidence of my nighttime adventure. I'll figure out a way to hide the holes in my wall tomorrow. I dry my hands and see my face in the mirror. My dark eyes are smiling.

That was terrifying, but . . . it was also amazing! I've never done anything like it before. How could I have? I was always locked in my room.

For a minute, I sit on the edge of the tub, staring down at the ugly bathroom rug decorated with roosters, and think. I'm sure I know what's going on. That British guy must be connected to the old lady who warned me to "mind my own affairs." They go into the empty apartment, but only at night.

Why? Because they're looking for something, and they don't want anyone to know about it. Maybe they're stealing that stuff. Those paintings might be valuable.

In my room, I snuggle back under the covers. I'm smug, self-satisfied, exhilarated. I know a secret. And I can get back into that apartment any time I want.

Maybe I can find what they're looking for.

Eight

A soft knock at the door wakes me.

"Rosie?"

The bright sunlight piercing through the blinds stabs my eyeballs. *Why am I so tired?* Then I remember my adventure last night. I groan.

"Our painting lessons begin today!" Sylvie calls in her musical voice, as usual slowing her words for me. "We'll go outside, to paint *en plein air*, like your Impressionists."

My Impressionists? I think in a fog of blank confusion. I crack open the window and the morning air that flows in and rolls across my face smells like bread from the bakery down the street, layered with exhaust fumes and a mixture of wet leaves and the scent of the ocean. I gulp a few deeps breaths and wake up and it all comes back to me.

When I started to pretend I wanted to paint, I mentioned Impressionist artists. A lot. It was part of the act I created to convince my mother that I belonged at a summer art camp. I chose Impressionism because they didn't go for exact detail or realism. Easy, right? And tons of artists who painted like that lived here in Nice, where I found this awesome summer art exchange program. So, like Sylvie said, they're *my* Impressionists. I can't forget. I stand up and moan. I just want to sleep.

"*Vite*!" Sylvie calls through the door. Hurry. Her light footsteps fade away.

After a quick shower I pull my hair into a wet braid that hangs heavy down my back, and get dressed. There are purple smudges under my tired eyes. I trudge down the hall. I don't *want* to learn how to paint. Unfortunately, I have to. I've got to keep playing along with my charade, to make sure I can stay in my chosen home when summer ends.

Bring it on, Rosemary. This is it.

Sylvie is beaming and bouncing around the kitchen, gathering supplies and shoving them into a canvas backpack. Her hair is twined into a million tiny braids that flow down her back and she's wearing a coral-pink skirt that floats as she moves, a black t-shirt and a sparkling silver and shell necklace. To me, Sylvie looks like a living work of art, full of color and life.

She hoists the backpack and winks at me. "We go now, okay?" Sylvie says with a smile. She adds something about breakfast. I think she's saying she'll buy it later. I nod.

We head down the narrow stairs that lead to the shop, greet Émile, who waves us away, his nose in another cookbook, and move into the street that's already starting to feel like home. Tiny shops, a bit like Sylvie's, line our path, but one sells only stationary, another, furniture, and the next place is an internet café. We pass the bakery that sends so many delicious smells our way, a restaurant, and finally a church.

The scent of incense and candle wax wafts from its tall, open doors as we pass. The smell is warm and somehow mysterious. Through the doorway I catch a glimpse of deep blues, reds, and greens on a stained glass window, flickering candles, and rows of wooden pews. Then a woman emerges from the cool darkness of the church, clutching the hand of a little girl. The girl looks up at me with wide, dark eyes and pauses to stare. Without bothering to find out what's causing the holdup, the child's mother yanks the girl off her feet and drags her along behind. I stop where I am, watching them go, hearing the high pitched protest of the girl's voice, the deeper, scolding tones of her mother floating in my ears.

Then I turn to watch Sylvie as she floats ahead of me, still chattering like one of the bright finches that flit among the trees. Joy breaks over me like a wave of the ocean. I dive into it. My plan will work. It has to. I hustle to catch up with Sylvie.

We come up to a little restaurant called *La Banane de Guadaloupe*. I blink a couple of times as I read and try to translate in my head. "The Banana of Guadalupe"? Or is it, "The Guadeloupian Banana"? The restaurant's sign is a big banana (what else) and the color yellow is everywhere. Sylvie motions for me to wait. She pops into the restaurant and my heart starts to do a little tap dance. I'm alone again. Even if it's only for a few minutes here and there, it feels so incredible. I smile stupidly at a man who sweeps by, carrying a briefcase and jabbering into his cell phone. He gazes at me with surprise and nods his head before he hurries on with a confused expression. I laugh out loud.

Then, Sylvie is back with a paper-wrapped sandwich, which she presents to me. It's hot and smells sweet, kind of like . . . bananas?

"*Croque chocolat-banane*," Sylvie says, her eyes sparkling. The crunchy, grilled sandwich is filled with banana slices and bits of dark chocolate. It's heaven. Sylvie laughs and hugs me. "Ansel's favorite," she says. Then her face clouds and she turns away, pretending to rearrange the backpack, but she wasn't fast enough to hide the tears that glisten in her eyes.

I know why she cries. It's one more reason I chose her to be my new mom. Her son, Ansel, is dead. After he left for Paris, there was an accident. A car skidded on wet pavement and plowed into a group of art students sitting at a table outside a café. I read about it on Sylvie's blog.

Suddenly, it's hard to swallow.

Sylvie turns back, blinking tears away, smiling at me in a shaky sort of way. I smile back around a mouthful of mushy banana and we keep walking while I lick melted chocolate from my fingers, promising myself I'll make my plan work. Sylvie's son is one of my "keys." He's one of the reasons my plan came together. There's a hole in his mother's heart that I can fill. I have Ansel's room. Soon, I'll have his family, too.

I'm in no hurry for the art lesson, but soon the narrow street opens before us and we are suddenly in a huge open space: Place Massena, the main square of the city. My eyes take in blue sky, pink and white buildings, and green palm trees and shrubs and bushes, dotted with vivid splotches of orange, yellow, and fuchsia flowers. The pavement below my feet is a giant checkerboard of alternating black and white squares. If you're an artist, I guess it really is the perfect place to paint, like Sylvie says. Everything is a jumble of colors and shapes, warm with sunlight and the smell of growing things and ocean.

So I'm not surprised when Sylvie stops to place her backpack on the raised edge of a small fountain and pulls out a tiny square of canvas. I help her unfold a small wooden easel that sits at the right height when placed on the edge of the fountain. I sit down to watch my first "official" art lesson. Sylvie is smiling and opening tubes, squirting blobs of paint onto her palette. Then, she hands me a brush.

"*C'est pour toi*," she says with a twinkling smile. "For you."

The color drains out of the day. Everything is now black and white.

"Me?" I sputter.

Sylvie thrusts the paintbrush into my hand, laughing. "I'll watch and help if you need it, Rosie," she says in her careful French, always so slow, so clear, just for me. "There is much to see here. The sky, the ocean, the trees, the fountains, the people. Paint what your heart sees."

"But, I don't . . . I thought . . ." I splutter in English,

and then stop. My cheeks flood with warmth that has nothing to do with the hot Mediterranean sun overhead. So here is where the lies end. Here is where my plan crashes and burns to ashes. I was so sure she'd actually teach me how to paint before expecting me to do it on my own! But of course, she thinks I already know a lot about painting, because of the stolen pictures. Stupid, stupid, stupid!

There were only three paintings. A tiny cityscape that Jada's brother did a long time ago. A field of flowers painted by a stranger, which ended up at a Goodwill store. A self-portrait my Mom did in a college art class. I sent photos of them to Sylvie, claiming they were my own. I wanted to prove that I belonged here. With her, the painter, to study art.

Why did I think this would work?

A man walks by and tosses his cigarette butt into the fountain. It fizzles out with an angry hiss. I stare at it as it floats on the surface, bobs for a moment, and then disappears. I gulp, feeling like my own head is sinking under murky water. I don't know what to do! How do you even hold a paintbrush? Is there some "official" way to do that? I try to keep from hyperventilating. My lie is about to catch up with me and beat me to a pulp. Sylvie chatters about Monet and Cézanne, Impressionist artists, while my legs threaten to dissolve. My bones must be melting in the hot sun. What was I thinking? I was so sure that Sylvie would ease me into this whole "artist-thing," not hand me a brush and expect me to turn into a mini-Monet.

Sylvie seats herself a few feet away from me on the

edge of the fountain. She takes a sip from a water bottle and smiles at me. Her eyes gleam, and excitement shines in her face. She has another artist to mentor, like Ansel. Except I'm *not* like Ansel. I don't have a single artistic molecule in my body.

I look around in desperation. I have to do something. What do I paint? The square, the pink buildings, the silver tram whirring by? My eyes fall on a pole not far away, near the tram stop. At the top is what looks like a carved man kneeling down on a tiny platform, like he's meditating or something. There are several more of them, lining the edge of the checkerboard pavement along either side of the metal tracks. Pole guys. Should I paint *them*?

Sylvie notices where my gaze falls and her face glows. She points and chatters in an explosion of French like a cloudburst of sound and I do not understand a single word. Not one. And then she waits, and I'm supposed to answer. Great. I smile and duck my head toward my canvas, placing my chin in my hand like I'm deep in concentration. Sylvie laughs and stops talking. And I still have to paint. *Do it, Ro! Paint something! Anything!*

Forgetting the metal pole guys, I take a deep breath, dip my brush into a color that looks a bit like the color of the sky, and smear it across the top of the canvas. The blue is too dark, so I mix in a dab of white, and it turns milky gray. That doesn't work for the sky, so I decide to paint the base of another fountain I see nearby. I move the brush in a circle as I try to create the fountain's round shape and end up with something that looks like a large toilet. I dip the brush into more paint, but the brush accidentally touches another color, and suddenly my toilet fountain turns a muddy brown. I toy with the idea of "accidentally" pushing my easel into the fountain.

And then a dog barks, and a shrill woman's voice shouts, and I glance up to see a short, blonde woman guiding a greyhound that's almost as tall as she is on a leash. The woman wears a white dress with horizontal black stripes, and white leggings with vertical red stripes. Her white-blonde hair is braided, much like Sylvie's, but the braids are uneven and lumpy, bundled up into a tangle on the top of her head, like a pile of frayed rope.

The woman lets her dog off its leash and it bounds into the toilet/fountain I'd been trying to recreate, joyfully leaping and splashing in the water. Then the woman sits at the edge of the fountain, tosses a cigarette into the water, and lights another. I watch the light glint on the water as it splashes, and the haze of smoke that circles the woman's head, and then I notice that the woman is made up of shapes. She's a striped watermelon on red licorice legs. I'm so desperate at this point that I figure she's as good a subject as any for my painting. I dip my brush into more paint.

I start with the round bundle of rope that's her braided hair, and then try to paint her cantaloupe-shaped head. I paint her watermelon-stripey middle, and add two long red licorice ropes for skinny legs. While the woman lights a third cigarette I paint a chocolate-dog dancing in the fountain.

The woman's dog jumps out of the water and gets her all wet, and her screams can probably be heard all across town. I look over at Sylvie. She's enjoying the show. She glances at me and winks. I try to smile back, but I'm so terrified of what Sylvie will think when she sees my painting that I can't.

Instead, I look down and rummage in the box to find a smaller brush so I can paint tiny stripes on the watermelon-shaped dress. The figure is so flat, with no depth at all. I have no idea how to make her seem round. Everything on the canvas is flat. I dab more paint onto my fountain, and try to make it less toilet-like. I dab dots of white to make splashes of water that spray up in the air around the dancing chocolate-dog. Then I paint a tiny cigarette in the woman's hand.

I step back to survey my work. My stomach squeezes into a tiny ball. The painting is terrible. It's a joke. A watermelon with a cantaloupe for a head and a pile of ropes on top for hair, and red licorice for legs. Smoking a cigarette. This doesn't look anything like what Impressionists painted. Is it Modern Art?

"Ah," Sylvie sighs. I jump. I didn't know she was right behind me.

Something in her voice makes me look at her. She's studying my painting intently, holding her hand to her chin. I start to breathe funny. She knows. What was I thinking? I can't fool her, she's a real artist!

Then Sylvie throws her head back and laughs. "Ah, Rosie! What a wonderful way to see the world!" She switches to her halting English, "Your Impressionists would be . . . impressed!" She laughs at her little joke.

"*Merci*," I whisper. My throat is dry and my voice

cracks. I'm not relieved, like I thought I would be. My lie hurts, because Sylvie might actually believe it. Why do I feel this way? I swallow the painful lump in my throat. Isn't this what I wanted?

We walk back to Sylvie and Émile's apartment. My mind whirls with a parade of colors and brief images that flash in front of my eyes. A girl with sad, dark eyes. A watermelon-shaped woman. A fountain that looks like a toilet. I don't really watch where I'm going and nearly fall twice. I'm so nervous my heart is drumming fast. Understanding finally hits me and I know why I'm afraid. I faked it today during my art lesson. Somehow, Sylvie still thinks I'm an artist. But that's only today. What about tomorrow?

Nine

So far, I've snuck into the empty apartment three times this week. I can't tell whether the paintings are worth anything. How the heck would I know? Nobody hears me. Nothing happens. It's been anti-climactic. Anyway, I find that I'm worried about other things. Right now I'm obsessed with pretending to possess a creative soul.

When I enter the kitchen for breakfast this morning, I'm feeling pretty good about the latest masterpiece I hold in my hands. I've painted non-stop for the last four days. Last night I did a lake, a cabin, and tons of trees. Happy trees. I do it by watching that guy with big hair on YouTube. He's the one who used to have this painting show on TV back in the dark ages, like the eighties, maybe. He paints step by step, I watch and copy.

Late-rising Émile is still snoring, but Sylvie is sipping from a tiny cup and bouncing her foot on the floor. Her high-heeled slipper makes sharp little *tap tap tap* sounds. Her face lights up when I enter. Practically flying across the kitchen, she swipes the canvas from my hands and plunks it down on the counter without even looking at it.

"*Nature morte*!" she announces with what sounds like triumph in her voice.

What? Dead nature? While I'm trying to mentally translate, Sylvie takes my shoulders and marches me downstairs to the back of her shop, where there's a humongous easel and a gigantic canvas. In front of this horrifying setup is a bowl of fruit, with peaches and pears and grapes spilling all over the place, next to a cracked ceramic pitcher, bobbling on a wobbly table.

Dead nature. Still life. I get it.

"Today I would like to watch you paint, *chère*," Sylvie says, her eyes twinkling. Crud. I try to smile like I'm excited, but my lips won't cooperate.

"*Petit-dejeuner*?" I mumble. I'm not hungry for breakfast, I'm stalling. But Sylvie laughs and grabs something from the table by her cash register. She hands it to me. Another chocolate banana sandwich, wrapped in wax paper. It's still warm. For some reason, this makes my insides go all mushy. She got up early to get everything ready. She ran to that banana-restaurant to get me the sandwich I like and bring it back, nice and hot.

So I perch myself on the stool in front of the easel and eat, while Sylvie chatters. I feel a flash of surprise tinged with more than a little relief when she picks up the brush and actually starts to paint. While she does, she talks about how light and dark shades create form and space on the canvas. She tells me to think of what I'm going to paint as a group of shapes, like I did when I painted the watermelon woman. It kind of makes sense. I watch as Sylvie does a little color-mixing demonstration.

As I swallow the last of my sandwich, Sylvie hands me my brush. This time, she stays with me. She coaches me along, and shapes begin to appear on the canvas. A few smears of green and yellow merge and morph into something real before my eyes. All of a sudden, it looks like an actual pear! On impulse, I put an arm around Sylvie. She hugs me back, and we both laugh, looking at my painted fruit. A knot in my gut unties. My secret is safe! I faked it until I learned to paint.

Sylvie backs away and leaves me to work on my own. She putters around the shop, and I find myself excited to finish my painting. I'm really getting into it, mixing more colors, adding this and that, so time passes. I can't wait to tell Jada! Then, Sylvie makes a soft noise like a sigh, and I glance at her, startled. She's standing by her cash register holding a few bills in her hand, but she's looking at the screen of her phone with a little frown on her face. She glances up at me, and her lightning flash smile appears, but it doesn't reach her eyes. What is she looking at?

Pretending to need more paint, I head over to the box Sylvie keeps on a shelf close to the register. As I rummage through the half-squeezed tubes of every color imaginable, I manage to shoot a glance over Sylvie's shoulder before she puts her phone away. The tiny image of my stolen cityscape is on her screen. My heart drops to my torn canvas shoes. I didn't fool her like I thought I did.

The shell curtain over the shop door sweeps aside and Sylvie and I both turn to look. Then I feel even worse. Two people are staring at me. The first is Gavin. His black coffee eyes find mine. *Why is he still coming around?*

The second person is an old woman with sparse, white hair that barely covers her scalp. She's my upstairs neighbor, the old shuffle-step lady who warned me to mind my own business. A little caffeine-jolt of fear shoots through me. I grab a handful of paint tubes and scuttle back to my perch in front of the giant canvas so I can pretend to work.

"Good morning—"

"—What's up?"

They speak at the same time. The woman turns to glare at Gavin like he's an annoying bug she'd like to swat. At that moment I wish I could like her.

"Hello again, Gavin," Sylvie says. "Good morning, Madame . . .?"

"Mrs. Thackeray. We're neighbors," the old woman says in English.

Sylvie introduces herself and starts to introduce me as well, but Mrs. Thackeray cuts her off.

"And you, young lady?" she asks, gesturing to me. "What is your name?"

I forgot my phone, but I can play this game. I pat my throat apologetically, shrug. Sylvie completes her introduction, says my name, something about how I lost my voice. Gavin chuckles softly. I'd like to stab him in the eyeball with my paintbrush.

Despite the fact that I'd prefer to duck behind

the huge canvas in front of me and hide, I stare at the old woman to gauge her reaction. Her expression is weird. Something about it is calculating, but also partly condescending, like she finds herself in the presence of someone far inferior. Anger ignites inside me and burns my embarrassment away. I sit up straighter and refuse to drop my gaze. The old lady wears a squashed puff of plaid fabric posing as a hat on top of her wispy hair, and her cheeks are sunken, like she's sucking them in on purpose. Crimson lipstick is gunked up at the corners of her wrinkly mouth. Without thinking, I make a tiny grimace. Mrs. Thackeray's wrinkly face puckers even more, which I would not have thought possible. She finally turns away from me.

Keeping her back to me, she speaks with Sylvie in a low voice. When I catch something about selling paintings and drop my paintbrush, Mrs. Thackeray turns and glares at me. I know she doesn't want me listening in. At this, I hop down from my stool and move closer, pretending to look for more paint. This ends the conversation and Mrs. Thackeray moves to the door. But she pauses with her gnarled hand on the shell curtain, and turns back.

"Rosemary," she says, with a quavering old lady voice that still carries a tone of command.

I just look at her.

"Was that you outside my flat in the middle of the night?" she asks.

I shake my head "no," as fast as I can. So that's it. She knows it was me spying on her that night. Well, she can't prove it. Remembering that I'm supposed to be engrossed in my work, I grab the first brush I find. It has no paint on it, but I dab at the canvas and stare at it intently, like I don't want to be interrupted. My heart speeds up. Does she also think I'm the one who caused the noises inside the empty apartment that night the scary guy was looking for me?

"I must have been mistaken," the old woman says. At that point I risk a glance at her and then I can't look away. Her eyes are narrowed to slits and her head is tilted to the side. She's a shriveled snake, waiting to strike. I can't always tell what people are thinking from their expressions, but at this moment I easily read the suspicion in the woman's eyes. She doesn't believe me, and why should she? I *am* lying. I try to look back at her with wide open, innocent eyes, but I can't help the sudden nervous swallow that convulses my throat. Mrs. Thackeray smiles.

"I see," she says. She turns and moves in her elderly way, slow and bent, through the seashell curtain.

"I shall return soon, Sylvie, to show you my paintings. Good day." She ignores Gavin, which shows she possesses at least some good qualities.

"Wow," Gavin says with a chuckle. "Wonder who dug up that fossil?" He materializes in front of me, tossing a sand art bottle from one hand to the other. I can't help the little lurch my heart gives when his face is right before mine. I hate him, but he's so cute! I'm drawn to his full, curving lips, gorgeous smile, and dark, liquid eyes. I detest myself for still being attracted to him. Boys are so confusing. I try to grab the bottle from his grasp, but he holds it out of reach.

"So you're sneaking out in the middle of the night? I bet you're meeting your boyfriend to practice a little French kissing," he says with a wicked smile.

I detest every freckle on his pasty face. Gavin continues to grin at me while he tosses the bottle back and forth in his hands.

I'm dying for something cutting and clever to say.

Jealous, much? Or how about, *Wouldn't you like to know*?

No, the first one's better. I *so* wish I could do sarcasm. I roll my eyes in frustration and turn my back.

"Listen, I came here to ask y'all over for dinner at our place tomorrow," Gavin says, louder this time, wanting Sylvie to hear.

"Oh, that's so nice," Sylvie says as she bounces over. "Yes, thank you." She drapes an arm around my shoulder.

"Here's the address of our apartment." Gavin hands Sylvie a slip of paper.

"What?" I blurt, forgetting that I'm not supposed to speak out loud.

"We rented an apartment for the summer," Gavin drawls out in his southern accent. "It's not far. I bet we'll run into each other a lot," he says. Then he smiles at me.

The jerk.

"Later," he calls as the shell curtain clacks and sways behind him.

Sylvie says it's time for lunch. We lock the door and clomp up the stairs. Gavin is here for the summer. His mocking eyes and stupid smirking smile make me feel like I'm a side-show freak on display for his amusement.

He *seemed* like he was about to apologize after he made fun of how I said my name, but he didn't. He didn't have time, really, because I dropped that stupid bottle. But then, later at dinner, he was back to operating in full jerk mode.

I head to the rooster bathroom and splash more cold water on my face, like it's going to just wash everything away. Keeping my face buried in the fuzzy towel that smells like lavender, I breathe for a while. In, out, in, out. Find my feet. Try to forget about stuff. But I can't.

Gavin could have apologized to me today, in the shop, but he didn't.

As I enter the kitchen, Émile comes in through the front door. His shoulders slump in a tired, defeated way. Leaving my side, Sylvie rushes to him and they embrace and hold each other tight. I hear murmured words, Ansel's name. Émile must have gone to the cemetery. He and Sylvie have already visited it several times since I've been here, bringing flowers.

The two hold each other for so long that I start to back away from them. I should leave them alone. The air in the room feels ten degrees cooler. At this moment, I don't exist in their world. I'm paint on the wall or a plant stand, nothing but an inanimate object that forms part of the room. It's what my life *is.* I'm a mute member of the audience watching a live scene on stage, not one of the actors.

I move down the hall to my bedroom, but stop with my hand on the knob. I wasn't ever an actor in my own life before, but what about now?

Sylvie and Émile are grieving for their son. One of the reasons I chose them for my new family is because they need someone else to love.

So I need to do something!

I tiptoe to the fridge.

There's a platter of cold meats inside. I put it on the table, creeping so I don't make noise. Plates rattle a bit, but Sylvie and Émile don't look up from their whispered conversation. I cut cheese into uneven chunks; add a bowl of oranges to the table, bread, bottles of soda. Then I'm suddenly enfolded in a soft embrace as two pairs of arms encircle me. I'm no longer paint on the wall. Sylvie and Émile have pulled me into their world, and I'll do anything to stay inside its warmth.

Ten

What's she doing in there, J.?

A warm, salty breeze rustles the leaves of the potted lemon trees around me while I wait for Jada to answer.

That's where she keeps her dead boyfriends.

I laugh and the noise sends a tiny swallow winging away toward the setting sun. I love Jada's sense of humor. I love my new life and freedom, and this rooftop garden I found my first night here. No one ever comes up here when I do. Most of the time, the place is mine.

It's obvious.
She's stealing the paintings. You should tell.

While I breathe in the sweet, fresh air of my garden in the sky, I think about what Jada said. If I tell someone that Mrs. Thackeray is stealing the paintings next door, I'll have to tell them how I know that. I'll have to tell Sylvie and Émile that I broke open the door in the wall and ruined their son's murals.

All around me, green ivy climbs white trellises and flowers are everywhere. Bright blossoms explode color. Fuchsias and blues and sunshine yellows fill my brain. My life is so different now. I lived in an old black-and-white movie where I was the prisoner. I was the bad guy. Now, my life is in technicolor, and I'm the heroine. It has to stay that way.

I'm not saying anything, yet.

> I'm not totally sure that they're stealing anything.
> It looks suspicious but I want to wait.
> What if I'm wrong?

"Rosie?" Sylvie calls.

> Gotta go!

> Hugs, bestie!! Miss you. Bring it.

The air leaves my lungs and I can't fill them again.

I miss you, too, Jada. More than you can imagine because I don't know when I'll see you again.

Of course, I don't tell her that. My thumb hovers over the screen for a second, but then I switch off my phone.

I wish I could tell her everything. I wish I could come clean, but I know it's impossible. If I confess too soon, my bright, shining new life could blow up in my face.

Sylvie's head appears as she climbs the last few steps and emerges onto my rooftop garden.

"I thought you were here." She smiles and I scoot over and pat a spot next to me on the small marble bench. Sylvie sits and breathes out a sigh.

"I wanted to see the garden," she says, looking around her with wide eyes. "*C'est incroyable*. I knew I could have a box if I wanted, but, ah, well . . ." She gives that totally French shrug that says so much without any words and smiles at me.

"Then it's good that I came here to Nice," I say slowly, in French, still whispering, always struggling to get the sounds to behave as they fight to get out of my mouth. "I help you learn new things."

"*Absolument*," Sylvie says, beaming. She puts her arm around me and squeezes my shoulders. For a few moments, we say nothing else. We simply sit in a companionable silence, only broken by the twitter of birds all around and the muted rush of traffic below.

"*Ma chère*," Sylvie begins, pulling her arm away. "I want to talk to you about something."

Coldness settles into the pit of my stomach and everything around me is devoid of all sound, as if the world is holding its breath, waiting to hear what Sylvie will say. I hold my own breath; terrified I know what her words will be. I remember the way she looked at her phone yesterday. She knows I lied about being an artist, and I have no idea what I can possibly say to her to explain.

"I, eh, *ben*, I want to say, we, uh," Sylvie says in English, clearly struggling. Finally, she shrugs and says, "I must speak in French, *d'accord*?"

I nod, swallowing.

She begins, slowly at first, but speeds up right away. Her face is serious. I listen, my hands twisted together, trying to understand. The exchange students who stay with her are artists who come to study painting as well as to learn the French language. Sylvie was thrilled by the photos of the artwork I'd emailed with my application for the exchange program, but now my work is so different. I am hesitant, not confident as a painter.

"And so, you see, Rosie, why I wonder if something is wrong," Sylvie concludes, her brow furrowed.

She's worried? I stare into her face, hardly daring to hope. She doesn't think I'm lying, but that something is wrong. I can work this.

"I, well . . ." my words trail off as I struggle to form them. Sylvie reaches out to squeeze my arm.

"Problems with your mother?" she asks.

Relief engulfs me. The world that was so silent a moment ago suddenly comes to life. I hear birds chirping and whistling all around; the breeze off the ocean rustling the leaves of the surrounding trees.

I nod, and Sylvie's furrowed brow smooths.

"I wondered. She calls you so often, sends you messages all the time. She does not want her little girl so far away, I think." Sylvie rises and walks about the garden, trailing her fingers along a dark green vine. Then, she whirls to face me. "I will call her, and say that you are well, and happy. That's a good idea, no?" she says hurriedly, her face hopeful.

I leap to my feet and blurt, "No!"

Sylvie's eyebrows shoot up to her hairline. My mind races. What do I say? Sylvie will need to know why I don't want to go home at the end of the summer, and I've already been trying to figure when and how to tell her everything. I try to come up with the right words, but I'm stuck. I look helplessly into Sylvie's dark eyes.

"It is not unusual that girls your age do not get along with their parents," she finally says, slowly, as though she's thinking about each word. "Things are difficult between you and your mother?"

My mood rises. She's given me a starting point.

"Things are bad. Very, very bad," I say.

"What do you mean?" Sylvie asks, her brow once more puckered.

I measure my words carefully. "She never lets me do anything," I begin, then instantly regret it. I sound like any teenager, whining about parents who won't let her go to a concert five hundred miles away or stay out late on a school night. It's not like that at all.

"She worries about you," Sylvie says, moving closer, "because she loves you." She brushes a strand of hair off my face and tucks it behind my ear.

"She worries about me all the time," I begin, desperate to find the right words. "Morning, noon, and night."

"She is a mother, *ma chère*," Sylvie says. "Even when

my Ansel was grown, I thought about him all the time. You never stop loving your baby." She looks down, and the expression on her face is so sad it hurts me. I close my eyes and turn away. How can I explain that my mother's love for me isn't like Sylvie's love for Ansel? Mom's love is a kind of prison that I have to escape from. My life has always been one of confinement. Locked doors and bars on windows. Ansel's life was one of freedom. Sylvie and Émile never tried to keep him wrapped in cotton and tucked carefully away. There's no lock on the outside of his bedroom door.

Before I can say anything else, the muffled notes of the "Imperial March" play from my back pocket.

Sylvie laughs at this. She finds it funny that I use this song as my Mom's ringtone. Then, she waits, looking expectantly at me. She even makes a little gesture, prompting me to pick up. Trapped, I answer, remembering to whisper.

"Where are you?" Mom shouts. Her voice is cracked and her breathing ragged. "I called the camp again, but some man answered and he had no idea what I was talking about! He said there's no such thing as the Red Rock Youth Art Camp! Then, some woman got onto the phone and said that there *was* an art camp and that you couldn't come to the phone. Something is going on, Rosemary! *Where are you*?" she shouts.

"Mom, I—" the words catch in my throat. I look at Sylvie, who now looks back at me with worry etched onto her face. I know she can hear Mom's screaming. The entire building can probably hear it from my phone.

"I'm outside in the desert, painting," I splutter.

"DON'T LIE!" Mom screams. "That woman said you were asleep!"

A gentle hand rests on my shoulder, and Sylvie sweeps the phone from my fingers. Icy drops of fear trickle into my stomach. I try to grab the phone back, but Sylvie has already moved out of reach.

"You are, eh, Darla, no?" she begins in her halting, strongly accented English. "Do not worry, Rosemary is well. She is . . . happy here."

Sylvie winces and holds the phone away from her ear. I can hear everything that Mom shouts. Now she wants to know who Sylvie is, and who that guy was, and why he said there was no art camp, and what is going on? I hold my hand out for my phone; feeling like my heart is twisting inside me, feeling my freedom slipping away.

"I am Sylvie, yes? You know my name, of course," Sylvie says when Mom finally pauses to take a breath. "We are so glad you let Rosie come to us this summer, we love her!"

I try to snatch the phone away. Sylvie darts out of reach, holding her other hand up in a warning gesture, telling me to wait. I bite my lip and draw blood. I feel like I'm waiting for a bomb to drop.

"Yes, she paints," Sylvie says. "She learns to paint very well," she adds, looking at me with a twinkle in her eye. I have to look away. I turn my back and pull random leaves from a lemon tree and shred them, dropping the torn bits over the side of the building. So close. I was so close.

"No, no, Émile," Sylvie says, as though she's correcting

something Mom said. "Men do not know everything, you know?" Sylvie laughs softly at something Mom says. I no longer hear my mother's frantic, screaming voice. I remain where I am, back turned, but my hands fall still as I listen.

"Ah, you were worried about your daughter, I understand. I will tell her she must call you more. She must tell you what she is doing."

I'm still kind of freaked. I'm scared that I'm about to be discovered, but something has changed. I don't exactly know what's being said, since I can no longer hear Mom's long distance screeching, but Sylvie is still calm, speaking softly.

"Of course. Here she is," Sylvie finally says, handing me the phone. Her face is smooth, unmarred by worry or concern.

"I'm sorry, sweetie," Mom says, her voice rough. "It's only that you're too young to be this far away from me! Your art teacher sounds nice, and she said you really were out painting. I guess I panicked, honey. You have to be careful, baby! What if you got lost? No one would be able to understand you," she says, her voice bubbling with tears.

After I move a few more feet away from Sylvie so she won't hear how strange I sound when I talk, I mumble a few lame answers and fake promises and get Mom to hang up.

I stare at my now silent phone. She hung up? She still thinks I'm in Arizona? I look at Sylvie, who gazes back at me with a softness in her eyes that gives me hope. How much English does she actually understand? Apparently, not much.

Drawing in a shaky breath, I feel strangely elated. As dangerous as it was, the phone call showed Sylvie some of what I was trying to say, better than I ever could have with my own weak, ineffectual words. I look into Sylvie's dark eyes.

"I believe that I am beginning to understand. As you said, things are, shall we say, difficult with your mother, no?" she says with a tiny smile.

We stay up on the roof, talking long after the sun goes down. Well, Sylvie talks. I still whisper.

I tell her things I've never told anyone, though I don't spill everything. I don't mention my nightmares about the weird shadowy images or ordinary things that terrify me. Or that I'm locked in at night. I don't tell her that Zander helped me come up with a fake art camp so I could come here. But I tell her about my mother. How Mom chooses what I wear. How she schedules every second for me. How I've only ever had one friend, chosen for me by my mother. How I've never been completely alone.

"Never?" Sylvie breathes out.

"Never."

I can barely read Sylvie's face in the moonlight as I say this, but I can tell she's shocked. I give her a moment to let that sink in. If she weren't here I'd be shouting with joy right about now.

I don't hate my mother. It's just that our relationship is . . . I don't know. I have no words to describe it. Complicated? That doesn't even begin to describe it. I mean, there's that whole thing with Mom locking me in my room at night. Jada doesn't even know about it. Her wheelchair doesn't fit in the narrow hall that leads to my bedroom, so she's never seen the lock outside my door. I've never told her about it, and I won't tell Sylvie about it now, because it's just weird. Like the kind of oddball thing that causes people to call social services. And I've never wanted that.

Anyway, I know my mother loves me. She's only trying to protect me. I don't want her to get into any trouble. But I don't want to stay in her world anymore, either.

Lie Number Five: I am going home in September.

Truth: I don't plan to go home. Ever.

I just want to get away.

And I think it's going to work.

Eleven

The view from the window in front of me is a brick wall, only inches from the glass. I'm fully under-impressed by the apartment Gavin's parents rented for the summer. Along with the dismal view, the place is all shiny metal and sharp edges, like something from a sci-fi movie where everything in the future is made out of chrome. I hate it, and everything in me wishes I were back in Sylvie and Émile's happy blue kitchen where there are no English-speaking guys.

I can't pretend that I'm fascinated by what's on the other side of the glass, so I turn around and watch Émile try to teach Gavin to speak French.

"Say it again," Émile says. "*Je m'appelle.*"

Gavin says, "Jim apple." At least that's what it sounds like when it comes from his southern-fried mouth.

In only two seconds, Gavin has revealed how horrid his French is. He can't even say "my name is" without sounding like an idiot. I try not to smile but I can't help it. I throw a glance over at his mother, Mrs. French teacher. Two little frown lines are carved between her dark eyebrows. They deepen every time her son murders the French language.

Gavin notices my expression. His face goes blotchy and his eyes seem kind of hurt. I wish I'd hidden my smile. I brush the thought away like it's an annoying fly. Why should I care about hurting his feelings?

"Real southern barbecue," Phil calls from the kitchen to the rest of us, all squeezed together as we are in the tiny front room. "Hope y'all are hungry."

The meal goes well. Meaning, Gavin doesn't talk to me. As we eat, though, his dark eyes keep turning in my direction. If our eyes meet, he drops his gaze. The shredded pork with spicy sauce is insanely good, but I can't help wondering when Gavin will pounce. I expect him to do, well, *something*.

We finish the meal and return to the ugly front room, where the adults have wine and Gavin and I are given lemonade. Valerie turns to me.

"How is your throat, Rosemary?" she asks.

I shrug. I knew I couldn't keep this laryngitis thing up forever. I was planning to start talking more to Sylvie and Émile. Like, tomorrow.

Sylvie says something about taking me to a doctor, a possibility that hadn't occurred to me. A little jolt of alarm jabs my stomach. I sip my drink and mentally plan my sudden "recovery." I'll wake up in the morning with a voice. It's way past time. Émile has started to look at me funny every time I whisper.

Valerie grins and speaks to me in English. Her southern accent is all drawling vowels that drip honey. "Oh, I do hope you get your voice back soon. I know Gavin here would *love* to get to know you better. I could tell he was dying to talk to you." Her eyes sparkle.

I'd rather shove pins into my eyeballs.

I avoid everyone's gaze and take another sip of my lemonade.

"It's so nice that Gavin has someone his age to hang out with," Valerie adds. She pauses and sips her wine. "Maybe we all can get together more this summer."

She beams at me and I sort of smirk in her direction. *As if.* Then Sylvie suggests that we continue to speak French since both Gavin and I are trying to learn.

I adore the woman.

Gavin stares at me for a second or two. His eyes look serious. He leans forward.

"Help me out, okay?" he says in a soft voice. "I don't understand what they're saying. Will you translate for me?" He pats the sofa next to him and Émile obligingly slides over to make room for me. "You don't need to talk loud," Gavin adds.

He's wearing this solemn, innocent face, but I don't buy it. He's trying to trick me. His Mom likes it, though. Valerie beams at us like we're just the cutest thing ever, two kids flirting with each other.

Of course, the moment Gavin asks for help, the conversation around us dies. Sylvie, Émile, and Valerie are all staring at me. I finally plop down onto the sofa next to Gavin. I don't know where to look and can't figure out what to do with my hands.

"Uh," I whisper, stalling for a moment. Then, I shrug. I wasn't actually listening.

"Y'all just keep on talking," Gavin says.

But Valerie is sweetly certain that I want to flirt with her baby boy. She leans forward from her perch on a little ottoman and whispers in French, "We were talking about going to the Matisse Museum together." She sits back with a conspiratorial wink.

There's no way out of this one. They're all staring at me, waiting. So I turn to Gavin and whisper, "Matisse museum." The last word trips me up. Three syllables smash themselves together into two.

"Uh, what?" Gavin says, his brows meeting in the middle. He looks uncomfortable, but I'm certain it's part of his act.

I try again. "The museum," I repeat. But I'm so nervous the word doesn't come out any better this time.

Gavin is staring. He blinks a couple of times and his forehead is crinkled. "I'm sorry," he finally says, "but I can't understand what you're saying."

"The Matisse Museum, dear," Valerie interjects. She throws me a nervous glance, like she can't figure out what's wrong with me. It's a look I recognize. I mean, I see it all the time.

What it means is: something is wrong with this girl. She's not normal.

I don't dare risk a glance at Sylvie or Émile. What do they think? Do they understand what's happening?

"Are you all right, hon?" Valerie murmurs. Her face now wears a look I can't stand. Pity.

"Fine," I whisper. *Why won't they just keep talking?*

Gavin clears his throat. "She said she was fine. So, anyway, I was thinking that I'd like to try wind surfing. I saw someone doing that yesterday and it looked like a lot of fun."

Valerie ignores him and goes to sit on her little coffee table so that she's right in front of me. Our knees practically touch.

She reaches out for one of my hands.

"What's wrong, Rosemary?" she murmurs in her honeyed voice. "It's okay, sugar. You're with friends. You can tell us."

Is she serious? The woman's face is inches from mine. Her wine left tiny purple stains at the corners of her mouth. Her pretty face isn't as young as I'd first thought. The lines show through her makeup.

She squeezes my hand. I can't take it anymore! First, she practically forces her son on me, and then she puts on this drippy, sugary-sweet act of concern for poor little Rosemary? I tear my hand from her grasp and bolt to my feet. My sudden movement throws Valerie off balance and her glass of wine goes flying.

Shouting at the top of my voice, I scream a phrase that I've never used before. Oh, I've thought it. Many times. But today it flies out of my mouth before I can stop it. And the sounds twist themselves into a million knots as they leave my mouth. I made myself look totally stupid. Worse, I've just shown everyone in the room that

I'm a liar. Or that a miracle just occurred and cured my laryngitis.

The silence that settles is the squirming, prickly kind. Everybody shifts around in their seats. Something clatters in the kitchen. Sylvie's dark eyes are enormous. Émile looks sad. Valerie's mouth hangs open. A dark wine stain spreads over the carpet at her feet.

"She said she was fine, *Valerie,*" Gavin says, getting to his feet. He walks out of the room and heads down the hall. His voice is angry. "Just leave her alone."

Sylvie and Émile say it's time to go. I don't know what excuses they give. It doesn't really matter.

We walk in silence. My heart pounds and my lungs want to explode. We pass shops closing for the evening and the ugly red and yellow McDonald's that's like a splotch of neon paint in a pastel world. We pass palm trees and fountains and churches. There are teenagers on skateboards, lovers strolling hand in hand, old men playing cards. They all look at me; a scrawny teenage girl with long, dark hair and a face twisted with anger, and I hate them. I hate them because they don't know what it's like. They're all normal.

My French parents murmur goodnight and nothing more when I head to my room.

I don't stay put, though. Instead, I sneak through my wall and enter the apartment behind it. I don't know why. I just want to be alone there, breathing in the smell of forgotten things.

Maybe that will help me forget.

The bedroom draws me the most. I sit at the dressing

table and stare at the spotted mirror. The table is covered with combs, brushes, tiny boxes and bottles.

Out of nowhere, I hear my mother's voice.

You have to try harder, Rosemary.

Rage rips through me. I grab a bottle from the dressing table and throw it against the wall. It shatters beautifully, exploding all over the place, and yellow fluid trickles down the faded wallpaper as a heavy scent fills the faded room. I smirk with a sense of grim satisfaction, but almost as soon as I do, the smile slides off my face.

Sylvie and Émile discovered that something about me is not normal. They'll treat me differently from now on. That's one of the main reasons I hate being me. I had hoped, truly hoped, that somehow I could fake it in a new country. I could hide who I was; pretend I was nothing more than some normal girl trying to learn another language. I thought maybe they'd think the way I talked was "cute." *Oh, that's just Rosemary's funny American accent. Ha.*

The smell of the spilled perfume is choking me. I stand to go, but as I do my hand brushes against something on the table. Among the bottles, combs and boxes is a square bundle of papers, tied with a dark blue ribbon.

I pick them up. They're letters, yellow and brittle with age. I hold onto them for a moment, put them down, but then pick them up again. Who would miss them?

Back in Ansel's room, I check them out. The blue ribbon is so old it falls apart when I untie it. The paper feels fragile, and the handwriting is tiny, slanted, and hard to read. It's almost faded away in some spots. My French isn't all that good yet, but I try to decipher.

> Ma Chère Marguerite,
>
> How I miss you! Your eyes are jewels that gleam in the sunlight! Your lips are like petals of the reddest rose . . .

It's totally cringe-worthy. Not very original, either, but I settle down to read with my cell in hand, in case I need to translate any words. The guy goes on about the woman's beauty and calls her sweeter than a "*gâteau au fromage*," which has to mean cheesecake. *Really?*

I skip ahead a little, and then find a phrase I think I understand.

> Even when your words are weak, they are sweet to my ears, for your voice is like music.

Your words are "weak?" Is that supposed to be a compliment?

I read and re-read this sentence. *Am I wrong?* I search for the word in my translator app.

Faible means weak.

The woman who once lived in the forgotten apartment spoke with "weak" words. *What does that mean?*

I fall asleep with the letter in my hand.

Twelve

Sylvie and Émile don't say anything to me during breakfast, but I catch one or two little glances they throw at each other. We eat in silence.

When we finish, Sylvie says something about working in her studio. Émile asks me to go with him to do some shopping, so we head out to the tiny grocery store the next block over. I follow him with a little red basket. The place smells like rotten fruit. Wrinkling my nose, I wonder about "weak words," and when Sylvie and Émile are going to talk to me about last night.

An elderly woman with bristles on her chin brushes past me and murmurs, "Pardon." She openly stares at Émile as he peruses the canned goods. He sees her gawking, smiles and greets her warmly. She nods back with round eyes and her mouth hanging open. Émile catches my eye and winks. The bearded lady moves on, we look at the cheese, and Émile chooses a chunk of brie. I add it to the red basket. We check out the pasta aisle. The old lady's there. When she spots us she cranes her neck to get another look at the short, pale man beside me.

Take a picture, it'll last longer.

Jada's first words to me. The memory floods through me, bittersweet. Mom met Jada's mom at yoga class. They talked, they bonded, they decided their daughters would be perfect for each other. A couple of freaks. Mom brought me to Jada's house. There she sat, engulfed in this giant wheelchair, like a scrawny kid with a blonde ponytail who was being eaten alive by a plastic and metal alien from a lame sci-fi movie. I couldn't tear my eyes away from the drop of drool that collected on her chin. Her head whipped around, fast, and she glared. She started hitting the side of her skull against this red button attached to the wheelchair headrest. I thought she was having a seizure the way her body thrashed around. Then she said those words.

I remember the horrified pause. Mom's quick intake of breath, the wide-eyed look. But Jada's words made me laugh. I giggled, harder and harder, and Jada joined in. And we were friends from that moment on.

It would be the most awesome thing to say. Oh, how I wish I could do sarcastic remarks! But they require perfect timing and perfectly spoken words.

I lift my eyes to the ceiling in exasperation and can't believe what hits my eyeballs. Chubby cherubs. The ceiling in this grocery store is covered with fat, naked babies flying around a bunch of wispy clouds. I start to giggle. Once I start, I can't stop. We buy the brie, some twisty pasta, some chocolate. In the checkout line I shake with laughter.

Émile breaks open the chocolate bar as we walk back and shares it with me.

"I'm glad you're in a good mood," he says.

I don't answer. I swipe away humor-induced tears and munch as I walk. I'm *not* in a good mood. I just can't believe that my neighborhood grocery story has fat naked babies flying around on the ceiling. *I love France!*

"Do you know how Sylvie and I met?" Émile asks, totally out of the blue, while some guy on a motorcycle zips by and shouts something. I shake my head.

"I was at the beach," Émile says. "A group of kids started to make fun of me. You know, of my strange hair and eyes and skin. They called me names and threw sand and rocks."

Oh. I know why he's telling me this. This is how he and Sylvie decided they would approach their discussion of last night's occurrence with me. I guess they figure since Émile knows what it's like to be an oddball, he's the one to do the honors. I take another bite of chocolate and think about cherubs on the ceiling above the pasta aisle, but this time, it doesn't make me smile.

"Out of nowhere," Émile continues, "a woman wearing a blue sun hat ran up to us. She shouted at the boys and even grabbed one of them by his ear. You should have seen his face! She threw a few rocks after them as they ran, telling them they should know how it feels," he says. His eyes crinkle with amusement. "And then she turned to me, took off her hat, and I saw the most beautiful woman I'd ever seen in my life. I was embarrassed that she had seen the need to defend me," he says with a rueful expression.

We turn the corner and head toward Sylvie's shop. I wonder if I'm supposed to say something, but Émile keeps talking. "As this woman walked over to me, she tripped and fell. She'd twisted her ankle. So," he says, opening the shop door and motioning for me to go inside, "I picked her up and carried her to my car, and took her to the hospital."

My eyebrows shoot up. Did I understand? The thought of Émile, barely taller than I am, carrying the much taller Sylvie . . .

"I'm stronger than I appear," Émile finishes with a grin, reading my mind.

I laugh and Émile joins in.

"Many people stare at me," Émile says as we climb the stairs to the apartment. "Like that woman at the store. I don't mind. At the beach, years ago, if I had been a tall, handsome man . . ."

"You *are* handsome," Sylvie says, sweeping over to us. She kisses Émile and winks at me.

Émile places his groceries onto the counter, turns to me and puts his hand on my shoulder. He looks me in the eye.

"So, now you know how I met Sylvie," he says.

I love him for the things he doesn't say. I understand what he's trying to tell me. I'm grateful for the affection I read in his eyes but everything inside me still feels kind of twisted. Émile could have told those boys to go away. He has a power I don't have.

Part of the reason I came here was to be seen as a normal girl. I wanted *somebody* to think that I was. Last night ruined that for me.

"We love having you here, Rosie," Sylvie says as she puts the pasta into the cupboard. "What does it matter if you cannot speak clearly?"

It matters a lot, I want to tell her. *To me*. But I stay silent.

Some things would be way too hard to explain, even if I could talk like a normal person.

"Shall we paint, Rosie?" Sylvie asks, brushing her hands together. "It is time for another lesson, no?"

I look up at Sylvie's soft smile and try to return it. They think it's all good now that we've cleared the air. Sylvie gives me a squeeze before we clomp downstairs to her studio. She hands me an apron and as I tie it around my waist, I mull over what happened. It might actually be to my advantage. Sylvie and Émile could be that much easier to convince to keep me forever. Rosie, the poor girl who can't speak clearly, needs their help.

The blank canvas before me is no longer the frightening challenge it used to be. I might try to paint a naked baby with wings.

"Self-portraits," Sylvie says. She points to a mirror propped up nearby.

Oh. Well, whatever.

I decide to make a tiny admission. "I don't know how to paint people, yet," I say, wincing at my "weak" words and hoping that Sylvie understood me.

"I will help you, like before," she answers. "We'll start

with a quick drawing before we paint." And then we're making sketches on paper, drawing ovals for faces and adding dividing lines to help us know where the features should be. It's kind of cool to learn this. Before I know it, Sylvie says we're ready to start painting.

"Do not worry about being exact," she tells me as she squeezes paint onto her palette. "Like your Impressionists, Rosie, you do not have to recreate reality exactly as you see it. You paint how *you* see something. Today you paint how your reflection makes you feel. What would your portrait say about you? Understand?"

I nod and pick up my paintbrush. I have an idea. I'll show Sylvie and Émile how my reflection makes me feel. Boy, will I show them. Right here and now, they'll invite me to stay forever. Smiling, I choose random colors and squirt paint onto my own palette.

Émile pokes his head in and says something that makes Sylvie throw her head back to laugh. Then he leaves, and Sylvie starts singing a song. Every verse ends with, "and then I have a cigarette." I find this hilarious. We giggle together as we paint.

Sylvie chats on occasion, telling stories about different artists who have lived and worked around here, slapping paint onto the canvas in her sloppy manner, and I do my best to remember what I learned about the correct proportion of facial features. What I start with looks terrible, but I keep going. While Sylvie keeps chatting, I paint some brown roundish shapes for my eyes. Ugh. This is so bad. I still laugh. I paint a blob for my nose. Ew. But I tell myself it's okay, because it's not about what I see. It's about what I feel.

"Good morning."

The quavering words float to us from the direction of the shop, and I glance up, startled. Where is Sylvie? I wasn't aware that she'd left her studio.

"Ah, Mrs. Thackeray. Good morning to you," Sylvie responds, her voice coming from the shop as well. Seconds later, she's leading Mrs. Thackeray right into the studio, and what's worse, the old lady isn't alone.

"You remember our neighbor, Rosie?" Sylvie asks.

I nod, but Mrs. Thackeray barely acknowledges me. She points to the gaunt man next to her, and introduces him as her son, Thomas. He towers protectively over his tiny mother, hovering like her bodyguard. His wide-set eyes dart around the room, taking everything in. A dark mop of curly hair, touched with gray, sits on top of his head like a tangled cap. Though his body is lean, it's also solid, bulging with muscles. Mrs. Thackeray beams at her son and pats his arm.

"My son, Thomas. I'm so glad he's here. I don't know what I'd do without my Tommy," she says.

Thomas nods a greeting, glances once at Sylvie, and then his narrowed eyes rest on me, and I know who he is. Suddenly, I'm back in my hiding place behind the screen, trying not to breathe as this towering man searches the room, inches away from me. I take a breath and step back. His eyes narrow even more. I finally notice the small painting the man clutches in his big, bony hands. It's the portrait of a woman with short, dark hair and gleaming eyes. Sylvie places an easel in front of Thomas, and he sets the painting there.

I turn my back and pretend to work on my self-portrait, adding random blots here and there while I listen to the conversation behind me and pretend to breathe normally. First, I hear nothing but blather about the painting, which Mrs. T. says was in her family for years, by some marginally well-known artist. Where should she sell it, what does Sylvie think it would be worth? Thomas says nothing, but I swear I can feel his eyes on my back.

Trying to ignore everyone, I work on recreating what my hair looks like. At least, I try.

"Did you hear me, Rosemary?" Mrs. Thackeray's quivery old-lady voice says, causing me to whirl around with the brush still in my hand and splatter paint.

"I asked if you have noticed any strange noises during the night. Last night, we were certain we heard noises coming from the empty flat next to yours."

I shake my head.

"Thomas and I are rather concerned about vandals. We've considered calling the police."

"We *will* call the police the moment we hear any other strange noises in that flat," Thomas says in his gruff voice. I know his eyes are on me, but I can't meet his gaze. Instead, I look at his mother. Mrs. Thackeray's crinkly eyes stare into mine. I know I'm being warned.

Sylvie chatters in alarm and asks me if I've ever heard any noise coming from the other side of my bedroom wall. I catch a reaction in Mrs. Thackeray's shriveled face when she realizes that my bedroom is right on the other side of the empty flat. Her face hardens and her eyes bore into mine, but a moment later she turns back to Sylvie, the hardness smoothed away, her expression calm, polite. Heart in my throat, I turn back to my easel.

A dark slash cuts across the face of my self-portrait, right across the blob of a mouth. I must have done that when I whirled around. It's perfect. It's just what I'd planned to do. I wanted to paint that bad dream I had. I wanted to show Sylvie and Émile what it's like not to have a voice. I only wish that our "guests" weren't here right now, breathing down my neck.

Feeling the gaze of two pairs of eyes on my back, like tiny spiders crawling up and down, I lift my paintbrush. I'm going to act like I don't care that the old lady and her son are here. I have to act like I didn't lie to them. I add more dark paint to the slash across my portrait. Soon, my painted hair sweeps across my face and covers my mouth. Then the hair snakes itself around my painted neck. It's exactly like it was in my nightmare. I keep working. The spiders stop crawling up and down my back. Noises blur into a soft hush in the background.

I don't hear anyone approach until the gruff voice whispers in my ear.

"We'll be watching you, girlie."

A heartbeat later, Thomas straightens and turns around. "I'm admiring the girl's work," he says in a loud voice, stepping back from me. "Fascinating. Well, shall we go, Mum?"

Mrs. Thackeray gets up, groaning as she moves. Then, she shuffles closer.

"My goodness, child," she gasps. "What on earth are

you doing?"

Sylvie puts her hand to her mouth when she sees my painting. Thomas checks his watch like he's bored and looks out the window. I can't read Mrs. Thackeray's expression, but she stares at me for the longest time. No one speaks. The smell of wet paint hangs in the air, along with Mrs. Thackeray's flowery perfume. It's too sweet, exactly like something an old lady would wear. I feel light-headed. I can't deal with what just happened. Thomas warning me, Sylvie's reaction to my painting.

"Sylvie," I whisper. I didn't think she would be *that* upset.

She doesn't answer.

I have to flee the scene. I can't help it.

"I'm going for a walk," I mumble as I head out of the room.

At the doorway, I risk a quick glance back over my shoulder.

Mrs. Thackeray remains where she is, staring after me, while Thomas continues to gaze out the window.

Sylvie is still staring at my painting. A single tear trails down her cheek.

Thirteen

Thomas is watching me. I made Sylvie cry.

These two facts float around in my head. I try to make sense of them as I stare out at the water.

Sylvie feels sorry for me. That was the cause of her tears. Getting her sympathy was part of my plan, but . . . I sigh and dig my toes into the warm, rocky sand of the beach.

I didn't want to cause her pain. I didn't want to make her cry. I just wanted her to care enough to let me stay.

As for Thomas, well, I stuck my nose somewhere it didn't belong and now I have to answer for it. What do I do? If Thomas and his mother accuse me of breaking into the apartment, they'll ruin my plan.

A hot wind carries the smell of sunscreen. I watch tourists oil themselves and turn over so they broil evenly. I sit and sweat, waiting for Jada to answer my email. I need her help. Finally, she answers.

You gonna take swimming class with me after school? Your Mom says ok.

Jada's message is not what I expect. Nothing about the apartment, Gavin, and the letters I took. Nothing about Thomas's warning.

So what? I want to answer. That doesn't mean I'll take the class, simply because Mom said I could. How does Jada know I want to do it?

I'll let you know.

I feel like throwing my phone, but settle for tossing a small stone that I grab from the ground. The beaches of Nice are covered with round, smooth *galets*, as Sylvie calls them. She gathers them, polishes them and makes intricate mosaics. Sylvie can make anything beautiful, even using plain, gray rocks. Why is it that everything I make is so ugly?

I have to stop feeling sorry for myself. I'm like this because I'm upset with Jada. She didn't respond to my pleas for help *and* she asked Mom about the class before she asked me.

It's hot. I scratch sweaty, itchy skin and finally admit the truth. I'm not mad at Jada. I'm mad at myself. My best friend still doesn't know the whole truth. When do I tell her? And how?

Closing my eyes, I raise my face to the sun. I don't want to lose my only friend, but I had to make a choice: accept a life sentence in Mom Prison, and keep Jada in my world. Choose freedom and a new life, but ditch the best friend. Well maybe I'll still have her, but she won't be here, live and in person. She'll be thousands of miles away. It sucks.

The sun is burning my eyelids. Shading my eyes, I throw another galet into the gurgling ocean. My phone plays Rob Zombie, Jada's ringtone.

"Girlfriend! It's me!" she says.

"Jada!" Relief and guilt start a fist fight inside my chest.

"You take swimming with me?"

What do I say? I don't have the right words. I can't think. I wait too long to answer.

"Rosemary? You there?" Jada asks.

"Yes," I say, still not sure what to tell her, or how. Maybe it's time, but the right words don't come. I'm too scared.

"Sweet! Be fun!" she says.

She thinks I'm saying yes to swimming class. I don't correct her.

"I sent your Mom some photos I said were from you," Jada says, while I'm still trying to think of what to say to her.

"Photos? Of what?" I blurt.

Jada grunts with the effort it takes to put her words together. "Cactus and rocks and a cool statue."

"Oh."

I am a horrible human being. My best friend is lying to my mother. Jada is helping me keep this massive charade going where I pretend to be somewhere I'm not, and she doesn't even know I'm lying to *her*, too. I pick at my t-shirt and pull the fabric away from my sticky armpits. *Why is it so hot out here? I'm dying!*

"It looks like that *Cars* movie," Jada says. She's laughing so much I can hardly catch the synthesized words coming from her laptop.

"What does?" I ask like a total idiot.

"Sedona!" Jada finally says with a loud guffaw, the kind you hear in cartoons but don't expect from real people. I love her laugh. I am the lowest life form in the universe.

"Thanks," I add as an afterthought, which I only manage after clearing my throat a few times so Jada can't hear the tears in my voice. "You know, for sending the pictures."

"No problem. Mitch says hi," she adds. Mitch is her boyfriend.

"Hi back," I say, sighing.

Oh, the fun conversation we're having.

We chat for a few minutes. I don't tell her anything. I don't ask if she read my email. I don't ask for her advice. Jada does most of the talking. Mitch is visiting from his school and will spend Saturday with her. They're up late playing Zombie Killers IV. Tomorrow they'll watch old horror movies, drink chocolate milkshakes, and hold hands all day. Special. We finally say goodbye.

I toss another galet, trying to make it skip like I've seen people do on TV, but it plunges into the water with a wet plopping sound. Maybe it only works on lakes. Seagulls screech as they circle overhead, and white sails float over the expanse of turquoise in front of me, like dots on a big blue canvas. The waves make whooshing sounds. The heat makes me feel weak and almost dizzy. My hair feels so heavy. I don't know why I came here, except maybe because of Émile's story I had the beach on the brain. Or maybe one day I'll really hop on a ship and sail away. Where to, I don't know.

"Why, hello," a cheerful voice chirps in bubbly Southern English. It belongs to someone I know and don't really want to hear. Valerie.

I glance up at the woman, wrapped in a pink terrycloth cover-up. Phil follows, puffing and wheezing with beads of sweat on his balding head. Thankfully, I don't see Gavin.

I stand and brush sand from my jeans.

"Mind if we join you?" Phil says. His smile is fake.

Yes, I do mind. Just keep on walking, hillbillies.

But I shake my head no, because that's what I do. I pretend. I stay on my feet. Phil places a folding chair on the pebble-filled sand and Valerie sits with a sigh.

"Such rocky beaches, here," she says, smiling.

Again, I move my head, this time nodding in agreement.

Then silence, except for the whisper of the waves. I scratch at an itchy spot on my head, wondering if I should turn and walk away, but then Valerie speaks.

"Hon," she says, with that sugary voice I now hate. Phil gazes out at the white dots of sails on the water.

"My niece has a problem, too. Not like yours, but . . . anyway, she stutters. She goes to a speech pathologist," Valerie announces, proudly, like it's a mark of honor in your family to need speech therapy.

I stare. How do I respond to that?

Phil clears his throat. Seagulls screech. Waves whoosh. Nobody says anything else for several seconds.

Oh, the fun conversation we're having.

"Um, I have to go," I mumble, and immediately feel the blood rush to my face. The words were mush.

"I have a date," I add in a rush. "Uh, I . . . don't want to be late." I'm glad the words came out clear enough, but why did I have to make them rhyme? *Who am I, Dr. Seuss?* I'm still flushed, partly from the heat but mostly from embarrassment at how stupid I always sound.

"Oh, you have a date? How nice," Valerie says. The look on Phil's face is one of mild perplexity. Either he didn't understand me, or he's shocked that someone like me could have gotten a date.

I throw them a lame, weak little wave of my hand while I turn to walk away. Valerie and Phil say goodbye with obvious relief in their voices. They won't be forced to endure a strained, embarrassed attempt at conversation with a girl who chews up all her sounds and spits out big wads of mangled words. My tennis shoes slide around on the galets as I make a non-graceful exit, happy that at least I'm escaping Val and Phil.

Shops blur past as I meander, not in any hurry. When I walk by "*La Banane*," a wonderful, sweet smell wafts over and I'm suddenly dying for another grilled banana sandwich.

The tiny place is filled with people. I join the long line. While I wait, I can listen in to what everyone else is saying, and I can practice in my head. I'll know exactly what to say and how to say it when it's my turn. The thought gives me just enough courage to stay.

And my words don't have to be perfect. I listen to some British tourists laugh as they try to order in French. The woman behind the counter laughs with them, but she's kind. She helps them and gives them their sandwiches.

I can do this.

I say the words to myself, chewing them, tasting them. I feel my tongue move, forming silent sounds, over and over. And before I know it, it's my turn, and I look up at the woman behind the counter and open my mouth to speak, but before I do she turns and calls out, "Andreas!" She ducks into a doorway behind her. Andreas emerges. He stands before the cash register, looks at me, and waits.

I open my mouth to speak, but nothing comes out at first, probably because of the boy's eyes. They are melted amber, surrounded by a fringe of the longest, blackest eyelashes I've ever seen on anyone, girl or guy. He has high cheekbones, honey-colored skin, glossy, dark hair. He says something and I stare at his mouth. I even think his lips are beautiful. And I don't remember what I want.

He raises his perfectly shaped brows above his gorgeous eyes. "What do you want?"

"Uh, I—" I start to say. I panic. I swallow nervously, while the young man taps his fingers on the counter in front of him, and I can tell he's getting impatient. So are the people behind me.

"*Croque banane*!" I blurt. I skipped a word. "*Chocolat*!" I practically scream.

My words didn't sound like French, or English, or any other language I recognize.

Andreas looks down at me. His forehead is wrinkled with confusion. He asks me to repeat myself. I try to speak, but can't. My tongue is glued to the roof of my mouth.

Before I can think of what to do, a man behind me shouts out something and shoves his arm past me. Andreas turns and takes a sandwich from the case beside him, hands it to the man and takes his money. I step back, shocked.

But my mouth is still glued shut. And then a woman orders something, and Andreas helps her. And then he helps another person, and another, and another. Gradually, I'm pushed aside and away from the counter. Andreas doesn't even look at me. Not once. I feel burning, stinging blood flood my face. I shove my way outside.

He didn't understand me. Why did I think life would be any different for me in France? It doesn't matter if I speak English, or French, or Swahili, or Pig Latin. I'll never be able to say anything correctly. I'll always be a freak.

Fourteen

J. You there?

She doesn't answer. I just wanted to hear her voice. I wasn't about to tell her what happened. I know what she'd say.

Hashtag so not impressed. Or *Hashtag bring it, girl*!

Jada, a major Twitter fan, started using that stupid word "hashtag" before practically every other sentence last year. She thinks it's funny. I did at first, until this guy named Crey Lewis started using it every time he saw me in the halls between classes.

Hashtag Mama's girl walking.

Hashtag mutation at four o'clock.

Hashtag Silent Hill.

I didn't get that one until Jada showed me a picture of a girl with no mouth. She understood the reference because her mother doesn't control what video games she plays like mine does.

That last comment bothered me more than the others, because it's true. I'm the girl with no voice.

I'm actually hungry now. I try to ignore my stomach, but I can't. So, instead, I sit and feel sorry for myself. Apparently, the only way I'll get food is if someone mistakes me for a garbage can and tosses their leftovers in my direction.

After I finish my pity party, I try to figure out what happened. I'm mortified by what went on at the sandwich shop. Why didn't I stand up for myself? What was I afraid of?

Two old men on a nearby bench toss crumbs to tiny swallows that hop and peck without fear at their feet. One even flutters up to land on the outstretched palm of one man, who twitters and chirps to the bird, like he's talking to it. Then, the man glances up and catches my eye. His eyes crinkle as he smiles and he speaks. I catch a few words, something about lunch time, but look away quickly and shake my head like I understood nothing when I really did.

I know what I'm afraid of. That fear is always with me. I'm scared I'll get the funny looks and the sideways glances. I don't want to see the faces wrinkled in confusion, the annoyance, the impatience, or the expressions of dawning comprehension when people learn that I can't speak correctly.

Hashtag hate being me.

More and more people head out to enjoy the sunshine, and I walk aimlessly among them. My stomach growls again when I pass a little outdoor food stand. I recognize *socca*, a thin kind of pancake made from chickpeas that Nice is famous for. I practically drool. The seller, an older stocky man whose square body is covered with a greasy apron, looks up and catches my eye. He grins a jack o'lantern smile and says, "*Deux euros*," holding up two fingers.

It's easy to buy stuff when you don't have to talk.

I should have thought of that in the sandwich shop. Just point to something.

I hand the man my money, and he hands me the socca. It's salty, has a nutty flavor, and it's hot. I inhale it right there by the stand, and buy another by wordlessly handing the man two more euros. I munch as I walk. With food in my belly, my mood lifts just enough that I'm ready to go back to Sylvie and my self portrait.

Then, something in a shop window hits my eyes and I freeze. It's the portrait Mrs. Thackeray was showing Sylvie earlier this morning, on display behind the glass. The shop is the kind with bars on the door. Something prickles in my brain. I hadn't caught everything that was said this morning, but I do remember hearing Mrs. Thackeray say that she wasn't going to sell this painting right away. And yet, only hours later, that very portrait is on sale in some snooty shop. I chew my socca without tasting it. Mrs. T. and her son didn't come for advice. They showed up with only one thing in mind: to give me their warning.

The painted woman beams at me from behind the glass. Her dark hair curls around her ears and neck, and her eyes shine, like she's been laughing at something.

I wonder . . . Could she be the woman who lived in the dusty apartment? Marguerite from the letters, the one with the "weak" words?

A dark form appears on the glass and floats up like a ghost to fill the space of the shop window. It's Mrs. Thackeray's son, Thomas. Our eyes meet. His are not friendly.

I turn and speed walk down the street, wanting to put distance between myself and the shop as fast as I can.

The shop door slams into the side of the building as Thomas flings it open. Then, his familiar gruff voice shouts, "Hey!"

I walk faster.

"You, there! Kid! Wait up!"

Yeah, right.

I pass a little alley and duck in there, but it's a dead end, so I pivot and come back out again. He's closing the distance between us quickly.

"Hey! Stop!" he yells.

I worm myself into a group of Italian-speaking teenage girls. They exclaim in surprise as I try to disappear among them, but I can't shake this guy. Thomas plows through the group like a big British bowling ball, knocking the girls aside, and he grabs me by my braid.

"Let go!" I scream. Terror shoots through me.

"We need to talk, girlie," Thomas growls. The Italian girls yell angry words at him, but he pays them no attention. He lets go of my hair but grips my arm and yanks me over to the side of the street. I drop my *socca.*

"I don't know what you're up to, but you stay out of

that apartment," the man says, grating the words out with his face only inches from mine. His eyes are bloodshot, and his breath is sour.

I'm so terrified I can't say anything. I try to pull away, but his grip is too tight. My arm is nearly numb, but then Thomas stumbles back and lets go.

"Ow!" he shouts.

Two of the Italian girls are slamming their heavy backpacks into him. Thomas holds his arms over his face in defense. More of their friends join in, shouting in shrill voices as they slug him with purses and tote bags.

A man runs out from a nearby bakery, shouting something in a shrill voice. Then, the girls all talk at once, gesturing and pointing at Thomas, who by this time has gotten away and is hurrying down the street. He glances back, once, and his face is an ugly grimace.

The girls swarm around me. They pat my shoulder, offer me bottles of water, and chatter words I can't understand. The bakery guy asks me who Thomas was, and I shrug. He stares down the street in the direction Thomas ran, shaking his head in disgust. I don't get away until we've all been given free pastries, little squares of puffy bread with bits of chocolate inside. I'm not hungry anymore, but I take my pastry and smile.

My scalp still aches where Thomas yanked on my braid. I rub my head as I walk home on shaky legs, afraid I'm going to meet his ugly face every time I turn the corner. He lives upstairs from me. What am I going to do? My brain buzzes with so many confusing thoughts I hardly see where I'm going. I collapse onto a bench and stare at discarded candy wrappers and bits of newspaper and string that litter the gutter. I add my pastry to the pile. And then, I let my hopes hurtle toward the ground.

I can't do this. Why did I think it was a good idea to come here to France? I can't just pick up and move to another country to ditch my mother and my old life. I'm fifteen, not twenty! How stupid was I to think this had even the slightest chance of working? I sit and watch people walk by. Most of them talk on cell phones or chatter in small groups. It's so, so easy for everyone. Everyone but me.

After a minute or two, I take a deep breath and grimace. The air around here stinks. It's like a thousand skunks paraded by and sprayed in unison. When I turn around I discover the source of the stench. I've been sitting in front of a beauty salon, and somebody got a perm.

The perm victim is an elderly woman who sits and reads while she waits for the chemicals to fry her hair. Neat rows of tiny pink curlers cover her head. A tall girl, the stylist, sweeps up a pile of dark hair from the floor. I imagine my own hair floating downward until the tiles below are covered with a scattering of black fuzz that piles up higher and higher.

My phone beeps. I get a text.

Hey, sweetie. U there?

I no longer see the scene in front of me. Only myself, silent and staring into the spotted bathroom mirror. Mom is behind me, combing, fussing, yanking, curling, braiding.

Adding ribbons or tiny bows with polka dots. Adding flowers. She did my hair every morning, right up until the day I left.

I'm fifteen, not five.

Rosemary?

I have to do this. I won't ever go back to my old life.

Hashtag Mama's girl is gone.

The handle of the salon door feels cool to my fingers. My heart speeds up. I enter and find myself smiling at the stylist. She has an eyebrow ring and pink streaks in her hair. She smiles back. Maybe I can't manage my mangled words, but I know how to point to pictures in magazines.

"Rosie! Your hair!" Sylvie gasps when I walk through the front door.

It's nearly gone. Yes, it is. I run my fingers through my gloriously short hair and grin, feeling weightless, like a cork floating in the ocean. Feeling free.

Sorry, Mom.

I don't need you to do my hair anymore.

Sorry, Thomas.

Let's see you try to grab me by my braid now.

Fifteen

Dear Rosemary,

I miss you so much. Please write back soon! It's dull here without you. Zander takes me out almost every night and keeps me busy, but I think of you every second. Are you still practicing? Don't forget, thirty minutes a day, at least! Have you made any friends? Remember that I love you to the moon and back.

Mom

I love you, too, Mom. But is it harsh if I say that it's easier for me to love you now that we're like, 5,468 miles apart? Maybe. It's true, though.

Dear Rosemary,

How's Paris? Sounds like you're having a blast. I'm proud of you, kid. I knew this would be good for you, or I wouldn't have helped you pull one over on Darla in such a big way. This is hard for her, so I planned a trip of my own. We're going to pick you up in August. A vacation in Paris should help her get over the deceit once she learns the truth (I hope). Anyway, I'm buttering her up by taking her out a lot. Glad to hear you liked the Louvre, but don't forget the Musée D'Orsay. It's my favorite, and that's where you'll find all your Impressionists.

Zander

PS

Don't forget to contact your Mom every day. She needs to hear from you.

Oh, Zander. You don't know how much I owe you. And how I'll always be grateful for what you helped me do. Don't hate me when I disappear from your life.

That vacation isn't going to happen, by the way.

Hey, Ro!

Your Mom is psycho! Yesterday she freaked and said she was getting on a plane to Arizona! Zander talked her out

> of it. He was like, "you have to cut the strings," or something. Or was it leash? I LOLed so hard. They would both freak if they knew what's going on. Thanks for your pictures. I love the pole guys!
>
> Huggies,
> Jada

So how much would you *freak, Jada, if I called you right now and told you the entire story? Would you still be LOLing?*

I bite my lip. I have to tell Jada some time, but I can't right now, in the middle of dinner while we sit at some café and people-watch. I shove my phone into my pocket and try to breathe slower. If Zan is planning a Paris getaway in August, I'd better get busy and work on the "I need you, Sylvie and Émile, to be my new family" angle, and fast.

People stroll by in the soft summer twilight, clearly out to see and be seen, chatting, laughing, eating ice cream, breathing in the sea air and the perfume of flowers and citrus trees. We're having a "special dinner to celebrate." Sylvie was thrilled by what I did, though I'm not totally sure why, since I didn't catch everything she said in her enthusiastic, bubbly-fast French. So now we perch on tiny metal chairs that surround a cloth covered table, sharing bread, goat cheese coated with herbs, and a salad of chopped vegetables with lots of olives.

"Your portrait, Rosie," Sylvie begins, once the eating slows down. She places her napkin onto the table and puts her chin in her hands.

"I didn't mean to make you sad," I blurt. I wince. Why can't I talk normally like everyone else?

"Ah, no, Rosie!" Émile says. He puts his hand on my shoulder.

"You do not need to apologize to us," Sylvie tells me. Her eyes are so sad. "I wanted to say how sorry I am for making you feel so, so . . ."

Warm relief floods me inside. I'm glad that Sylvie wasn't too upset by my painting. She was only worried about me, which is what I wanted in the first place.

"Sylvie!" a woman calls. "Émile!"

We all turn as a woman with curly auburn hair weaves her way through the tables toward us. She's an exclamation point of a person, nothing but long, long legs, like she follows a diet of celery sticks and air. Heads swivel, whispers start and eyes follow her as she hurries right up to our table.

"Nicole!" my French parents both call out. They rise to greet her with warm hugs.

My pulse quickens. I know her! Her face is on magazine covers and billboards. But can she be the very same Nicole I learned about on Sylvie's blog? Based on Sylvie's tears and the expression of joy that broke out on Émile's face, she must be. Ten years ago, before Ansel died, Nicole had nowhere to go. Sylvie and Émile took her in. She was fifteen, like I am now. Her story, her very existence gave me the courage to try something crazy.

This is too perfect.

I am introduced. I mumble an awkward greeting but

am soon at ease with Nicole, with her gleaming hazel eyes and ready smile. She gives me a hug when she learns I'm staying with her former family.

Émile orders dessert. While I sip Orangina, I sit back and listen. Nicole speaks in rapid French I can barely follow. She was passing through Nice, had stopped by and was disappointed not to find her dear friends at home, but voilà! Here they are!

Her joyful mood is infectious. People around us turn to stare and pull out their phones to take quick photos when they think Nicole isn't looking. She pays it no mind. Warmth spreads through me. Nicole was just what I needed. She is my shot of courage. There's no way I'm giving up on my plan, because it will work.

Over a tray of pastries, we laugh at nothing and everything. I even manage to answer a couple of questions, speaking softly. Sylvie beams, Émile's indigo eyes gleam. Nicole doesn't bat an eye when I screw up my words and sound weird.

Ansel's name is mentioned. The mood grows darker in an instant.

Sylvie wipes her eyes. Émile touches her face once, gently.

"I miss my baby," Sylvie whispers down to her plate. Nicole hugs her.

"I'm sorry," I say, at a loss for words, this time not out of fear that I won't be understood, but because I know there are no words in any language that would ease Sylvie's pain. My pulse quickens, then, at the thought that I need to take advantage of this moment, when Sylvie and

Émile are reminded so sharply of their own loss. I need to let them know that I can fill the void in their lives. Like Nicole, I can be a daughter to them. Then, guilt sweeps through me that I could be so unfeeling and selfish at such a moment.

But Émile and Sylvie's loss was one of the biggest reasons I chose them as my host family. I think of Sylvie's blog. All her posts about Ansel. How he would endlessly draw and paint, get in trouble at school for doodling instead of listening. How he once cut his own hair. That's it!

"Sylvie," I say, clearing my throat. I try to ignore the guilt that rises from my stomach. "Tell me about Ansel. You said once that he, um, cut his hair?" I'm not sure of the French words I'm using, so I make gestures with my fingers, pretending they're scissors, snipping at my shortened curls. "You were angry?" My words aren't too clear, but I'm growing used to speaking in front of my French family, especially now that they know about my speech problems. And Nicole is so kind.

I'm rewarded by a chuckle from Émile and a watery smile from Sylvie. Nicole beams at me while Sylvie reaches out to touch my own newly shorn head, and tells me in a wavering voice of the time Ansel, only thirteen, used his father's razor to shave himself bald. Then, horrified at the result, he'd begged his mother to buy him a wig. We all laugh together. I shove my guilt down to some place where I can hardly feel it.

Nicole takes her leave. She embraces Sylvie, Émile, even me. Then she asks for my cell phone and types in her phone number and email while I stare in shock. She tells me that she wants to correspond. She lives in London, now. She even says something about how I should come to visit her.

I stare at her as she walks away, along with everyone else who happens to be in the vicinity. Did I just make a friend? On my own? I curl my fingers around the cell phone in my pocket. For the first time in my life, I have more than three people on my contacts list.

We join the throng of tourists and locals on the Promenade des Anglais, walking along the shore. The summer twilight has a mellow quality, making everything glow softly as if lit from within. I'm on this weird high, thrilled by the promise of friendship with Nicole. I don't care that she's super-famous or celery-stick thin. Nicole, one of Sylvie and Émile's "strays," like me, treated me like I was normal. I will never forget that.

As we walk, I try to keep Sylvie and Émile talking about Ansel. Once, when I say how much I would like to have known him, a strange expression glimmers in Émile's eyes, but then it's gone, and he tells me how much he thinks Ansel would like me. Sylvie beams at this and nods. She hugs me to her, whispering, "I would love to have a daughter like you." I hug her back and inside I'm flying. It's working!

We buy apricot sorbets and continue to stroll, each now silent, wrapped in our own thoughts. I'm dizzy with the hope that rises inside me. I taste my tart sorbet, listen to the musical shuffling and murmuring of people passing by, and breathe the smells of a city by the sea: vehicle exhaust, green growing things, and fishy ocean air. My short hair tickles the back of my neck, and I shake my head, loving the feel of weightlessness. A burden lifted.

Up ahead, neon pink, blue, green, and yellow lights glow high above, bright dots that float in the darkening air as we stroll toward the square. I point at them and am relieved when I don't have to ask what they are, because Émile, wonderful Émile, understands my unspoken question.

"The statues on poles near the tram stop. I am certain you have seen them, yes?"

I nod. So the kneeling pole guys light up at night? Weird. A laugh bubbles up and I giggle out loud. The thought of the funny statues glowing in the dark like giant night-lights for grownups cracks me up. Émile opens his mouth like he's about to say more, but then he closes his lips and simply grins and pats my shoulder. I smile at people I don't know. As we head away from the shore and onto the gently sloping hills of the city, passing through the narrow streets that wind between low stucco buildings, I already feel at home. It's a sense of familiarity and of belonging. A sense of safety. Not the kind of safety behind locked doors, but the kind that's open and free.

Then, a tall man pushes his way past us, ignoring Émile's startled exclamations, and I gasp and almost choke. The shoving man turns back for a brief moment, giving me enough time to see who it is. Thomas! Instinctively, I shrink behind Émile and Sylvie, who both glare at the man's fading form.

"Rude," Émile murmurs. He and Sylvie continue on

their way, and I follow on shaky legs. My thoughts whirl as we head up the stairs to the apartment. The safety of my new home is a precarious, fragile one. When I went inside that empty apartment, I put everything, my new life, my new family, and my freedom, at risk. But now it's too late to undo what I did. How do I move forward from here and make my position in this family secure, when Big Scary Guy and Evil Old Lady are right upstairs, watching my every move?

Back at home, I find myself confiding in Fat Cat. He listens, snorts on occasion, purrs, but mostly stares with that unnerving, unwavering gaze that cats have.

Stay out of their way, he seems to say as he peers into my face. *That's all you have to do.*

But is that possible? I look up at Ansel's painted ceiling, even though it's dark and I can't see anything. I'm too worried to sleep. Maybe Jada will finally help me. It's morning for her. I'll send her another message. I want her to see my new look anyway. With tired fingers I type,

Check this out.

I upload a photo of my new look, find Jada's name on my list and hit *send*. When Jada answers, I'll tell her again about Mrs. Thackeray and her son, and ask her what to do. My phone rings immediately.

"Hey," I say, hearing the smile in my voice.

"Rosemary, your hair! Your beautiful hair," Mom's voice sobs in my ear.

Oh, crap. I chose the wrong name on my contacts list!

There are only four names to choose from. How could I be so brain dead I picked the wrong one? Air leaves my lungs and I can't fill them again.

"Hi, Mom," I croak.

Her voice booms in my ear, loud, insistent, and furious. It's 2:30 a.m. when she finally ends the call. I'm camped out on the floor with Fat Cat. He's out, breathing evenly. I'm wide awake and wired, like I've downed a case of forbidden Coke.

> Don't forget!
> I mean it. Send me something tomorrow.

It *is* tomorrow, Mom.

I consider typing that, but I don't.

> Got it.

The air inside my room is stale and warm, and smells like my dirty socks. I stretch out on the paint-splattered carpet. Faint light that comes through the blinds makes stripes on the wall. I count them about a million times, but I can't stop shaking.

My plan was to trash this phone and get a new one, but only after I convinced my French parents to keep me. I've been so busy faking artistic talent and breaking and entering that I haven't worked on this part as much as I should have. I felt great at dinner, like it was all coming together, but I haven't yet told Sylvie and Émile that I want to stay forever.

Sylvie said she'd love to have me for a daughter. But

when summer ends and I ask to stay forever, what will she say at that moment?

I pick up my phone. Photographed faces beam out at me from the screen. Jada and me. The two of us are together, smiling, our arms around each other. Mom, with her smothering love written all over her face. Zander, with his "old guy trying to look young" eyebrow ring. And no one else. Zander's the key. I wasn't sure I'd actually go through with it, but now I know that I will.

Lie Number Six: Zander is an evil man. He's doing something terrible to me.

Truth: Zander is the good guy everyone thinks he is. But they don't need to know that.

Curling up into a ball, I hug my legs and put my forehead down on my knees. *I'm sorry, Zan. But it can't hurt you. You'll never even know.*

Sylvie and Émile won't let me stay with them simply because I "don't get along well" with my Mom. Nicole had nowhere to go, but I do. I have a home to return to. But they might let me stay if, well, there's *something* going on between me and my Mom's boyfriend. Something very, very bad.

Sylvie and Émile are the perfect new family for me. They lost a child and have room in their lives for someone new. They take in strays, like Nicole, so it's not like they haven't done something like this before. But there's one more thing that makes this work so well. Sylvie used to lead a support group for girls, all victims of abuse. She was molested as a child. She writes about this in her blog, sharing her story with the hope that she can help others.

Sylvie will let me stay if she thinks I'm afraid of Zander.

Bring it, Rosemary. I take a deep breath. First, I'll throw Mom off my trail and do what she asks so my plan has time to work.

She wants a painting. Proof that this "art camp" thing was worth it. So, I'll send my mother a painting from "Arizona," and not just any painting. I need something fantastic, something that will convince her that I'm a real artist. I don't need her to become any more suspicious than she already is.

All is quiet next door. I creep inside, hardly daring to breathe. I find a small still life that reminds me of the dressing table in Marguerite's bedroom. There are irises in a glass vase and a jumble of containers and bottles on a table. All the objects are reflected in a mirror behind them. It was painted with lots of blues and purples and makes me think of twilight and cool air on skin. There's no artist's signature on the painting. Now it's mine.

A Rosemary original.

If they even miss it, my upstairs neighbors might suspect that I took it, but they'll have no proof.

Besides, I'm only taking one painting, from hundreds. Who's going to miss it?

Sixteen

"Here you are," Émile says as I enter the shop, yawning after my long night. Minutes ago, I successfully mailed a package to Benita, aka the "Art Camp Director," in Arizona. Helpful that Zander has a cousin who lives in Sedona. From her, the painting will get to Mom.

It was great that the guy behind the glass who helped me at the post office didn't even look at me. He just took the package, weighed it, and told me how much.

It's such a relief when I don't have to talk to anyone.

Émile smiles at me. "One of our neighbors asked me for help, and I told her you would be happy to do it," he says, gesturing toward the stairs. "Let's go."

Blinking as my eyes adjust to the dim light inside, I follow, smiling to myself, humming something tuneless, wordless, nothing more than happy notes that slide freely from my mouth. We climb, I hum. Émile leads me to the floor above ours. He knocks on the very first door and opens it without waiting for a response. I stop humming. It's the old lady's apartment.

What if Thomas is there?

Inside, the drapes are closed. A thick blackness hides everything from my eyes. Night time in Sylvie's apartment is somehow different. It's shades lighter than the suffocating daytime shadows that surround me here. Sylvie and Émile's home holds a feather-light darkness, waiting to be brushed aside. Mrs. Thackeray's place feels like it's full of secrets.

Someone coughs, and I hear movement. A single table lamp clicks on and I finally spy the crumpled up form of Mrs. Thackeray on the sofa. What was she doing, sitting there in the dark? Did she think that was some kind of dramatic entrance?

She points around the room. The dim yellow glow reveals a place almost as cluttered as the so-called empty apartment downstairs. Piles of books, boxes, clothing, and other objects crowd every available surface and spill out onto the floor.

"I am so grateful, dear Émile," Mrs. Thackeray says. Her voice surprises me. It's full of sweetness. "You can see how many things a silly old woman can accumulate during a lifetime. But, of course," she adds with a wheezy, rattling chuckle, "one must not hold on to the past forever. It's very kind of these young people to help."

Before I can wonder what she means by "these young people," Émile speaks.

"Ah, here he is. When he stopped by this morning I asked him to join us. *Merci*, Gavin."

Gavin walks in with his hands shoved into his pockets and his head down low. His face is wary, his eyes watchful. "Hey, Rosemary," he says.

I don't answer. Awkwardness ensues, as it always does when I'm around.

"Take as long as you need to," Émile says. The door clicks shut behind him.

Mrs. Thackeray speaks again. This time her voice is imperious and commanding. All the sugar has melted away.

"You may begin. These boxes must be taken downstairs to the truck parked on the street," she says. I get the feeling she's used to having people practically salute when she speaks.

"Sure," Gavin says. Then he turns to me. "I like your hair. It looks good." Is he being sarcastic? I feel my face flush and am grateful that the lighting in the room is barely adequate.

I could bail, but I don't. What would I tell Émile and Sylvie? What would Mrs. Thackeray say to them? My biggest fear is Thomas. What if he makes an appearance?

I swallow, find my feet, and breathe. I have to chill! It's to my advantage that I'm not alone. I may not like having Gavin around, but his presence is reassuring. So I'm actually glad he's here. Weird.

Gavin grabs a box, and I do the same and follow him back to the door, throwing a glance in the old lady's direction. I can tell she's staring at us, even though her face is shadowed. I hear another of her wheezy chuckles. My blood starts to simmer.

If that's how you want it, lady, game on.

Except I don't understand what the game actually is in the first place, but it's got to have something to do with the empty apartment. Do they know I just took one of the paintings?

We clomp down the stairs. My box is full of yellowed underwear and stained socks. The smell of old sweat and moth balls makes my stomach curl around my breakfast. Gavin gets so far ahead of me that I can't catch up with his long-legged gait until we're nearly outside.

"What *you* doing here?" I blurt at him when I reach him. My face flames when I realize I've left out a word. Gavin doesn't notice.

"My Dad and *Valerie*," he says, putting his usual sarcastic emphasis on his Mom's name, "told me that I needed to come by and apologize to you." He shoulders his way through the main doors and dumps his box onto a moving van parked on the street. Then he turns back and stares at me with his arms folded, leaning against the van.

"So, I'm sorry," he says. His mouth is in a tight line and his body is tense.

I stare at him for two reasons. One is that out here in the morning sunlight, I can clearly see his face. And his eyes aren't mocking, they aren't calculating. More than anything, they look sad. Two, he shouldn't be the one to apologize. Not really. It was his Mom who made everything so humiliating and horrifyingly awkward the other night. It was Valerie's fault.

"I," I start to say, then freeze. How do I tell him any of this? How can I get the right words out? I can't. I grimace and bite my lip, trying to think of what to say.

Gavin drops his gaze and sighs. "Whatever," he mumbles. Then he lopes back over to the front doors and disappears inside.

People don't realize how fast you have to talk to have a conversation. Jumbles of sounds fly out of your mouth in rapid succession and it's all totally automatic. I mean, it just happens and you don't even think about it. Unless you're someone like me.

When you have to consciously think about every single thing that's going to come from your lips, and never know if it will even come out right, talking is torture.

Communication is almost impossible.

I growl and follow Gavin. I don't want him to get ahead so that we're not in the apartment at the same time.

When we arrive at Mrs. Thackeray's home, Gavin opens the door for me. And his words shock me so that I stumble and nearly fall.

"Yeah, ice cream sounds great, Rosemary," he says in a loud voice as we enter. "But why don't we pack a lunch and head to the beach, first? It's a great day for a picnic."

He grabs a box and sprints out the door before I can answer. I snatch an armful of old coats and follow, fuming. Mrs. Thackeray is still perched on the sofa. Her feet dangle a few inches above the floor, making her look like some evil little troll child. I steal a glance at her as I pass. She's smiling. I stifle the urge to throw something at her head and stomp out into the hall.

Each time Gavin and I return to the apartment, he makes sure he gets ahead of me and announces something else as he opens the door.

"I'd love to teach you to surf! Love to see you in your new bikini, too!"

"I'm psyched I finally found a girl who wants a large family! Like, ten kids, you said?"

"I'll have to save for a few more years if you want a ring like *that*!"

Mrs. T. giggles at every comment. I'm surprised she doesn't start clapping. I'm dying to scream at the two of them, but I don't. I know what will happen if I do. Anger turns my words into sludge.

I hate him. And he still never apologized for what he did in the shop.

Finally, we wrangle the last boxes onto the truck and head back once more to Mrs. Thackeray's dark apartment. This time, I'm determined to beat Gavin at his own game. I manage to trip him on the stairs and sprint for Mrs. Thackeray's door, but he recovers too quickly and follows on my heels.

"Whoa, slow down," he pants once we get inside. "You're moving a little too fast for me. Oh, and you might want to fix your lip gloss," he adds with wicked grin.

There's no sound in the room. No wheezy chuckle, no appreciative audience. I blink, surprised that the tiny woman isn't here.

Gavin shrugs and turns to me. This time, he's no longer smiling and his face is defiant.

"What was that about?" I blurt, glad I manage to keep my temper in check. At least my words are clear. Kind of.

"Just teasing you," Gavin says, his eyes challenging.

"Not funny," I mumble.

"Then why didn't you say something?" Gavin demands, moving a step closer.

Because I can't, you idiot! Don't you understand that?

I shake my head and plant my hands on my hips. And glare.

Gavin's eyes narrow. "Forget it," he mumbles. "I'm out of here."

I watch him go, wanting him to stay but not knowing how to get him to do it. I don't know how to explain something to him that I don't totally understand myself. But I have to try.

"Wait," I say.

Gavin turns, hovering over the threshold.

And a sudden weight presses on my shoulder. A hand, with strong, bony fingers grips tight and doesn't let go.

"Not you, girlie. You're not done, yet."

I hadn't noticed Thomas in the shadows. I wrench myself from his grasp and step back. He glowers in my direction, but doesn't try to grab me again. Instead, he moves to the door and shoves it closed, pushing Gavin all the way outside. I hear a muffled "Hey!" from the hallway. Then, I hear the lock click. My heart leaps into my throat and tries to choke me. I've always had a problem with locked doors.

"They're waiting for me at home," I say with a shaking voice, looking up at the gaunt man before me. The words come out totally scrambled.

"What?" the man growls. I can't answer because my tongue is now frozen.

I step back when Thomas moves, but he doesn't come any closer to me. He simply stands against the locked door, arms crossed in front of his chest. Gavin pounds on the door from the outside. Thomas ignores him. Fear knifes my stomach. Now I know the reason for Mrs. Thackeray's little game. They wanted to get me here, alone, but make it look legit.

"How are you getting inside, Rosemary?" the old woman asks from behind me.

I whirl and there she is, once again settled into a corner of the couch like an overlarge, wrinkled pug. Where had she been? Her question doesn't surprise me, but my tongue is super-glued to the roof of my mouth. I'm afraid no words will ever come out again.

"Come on, then!" Thomas barks. "Answer her question!" The pounding on the door stops. Gavin has abandoned me.

"I—"

"Answer me!" Thomas shouts.

"Get in where?" I say. My voice is so quivery the words seem to shiver apart and fall to the floor.

"You know where!" Thomas roars. "Into that flat next to yours. We know you've been in there!"

"I don't know what you're talking about!" I scream. My words slur together like I'm drunk.

With a wordless growl, Thomas takes a step toward me.

Someone pounds again on the door, hard.

"Rosie?" Sylvie's voice calls. Her voice is shrill.

"Here!" I shout. Thomas glares at me, but he turns to

unlock the door and swings it wide.

Sylvie and Émile rush inside. I bolt over to them, finally able to breathe.

Everyone talks all at once, except for me. Sylvie shouts and gestures. Thomas manages to look insulted.

Mrs. Thackeray says we were chatting. She asks why in the world Sylvie is so upset. "We were about to invite Rosemary to stay for tea. We would have invited that nice young man, too, but he left."

"I want to go," I say to Sylvie. She leads me out with a strange look on her face. Émile stays behind in Mrs. Thackeray's apartment, saying something I don't catch. I flinch at the sound of Thomas's rumbling voice, as he answers. What if he tells them what he knows about me? What would I say? More lies. More and more lies. I'm shaking.

We descend the stairs, but at the bottom, Sylvie grabs my shoulders and turns me around to face her. Speaking in rapid French, she asks me if I'm really all right. What did he want? Why are you so frightened? Did he do something? Sylvie's face is hard. She's angry, but I also sense fear in her widened eyes. She is truly afraid for me.

My body won't stop trembling. This situation wasn't like what she's thinking, but I know why Sylvie reacts this way. What happened looked totally suspicious. Add to that the fact that I'm shaking in my sneakers. I *was* terrified when Thomas locked the door. It's how I feel every night when Mom shuts my door and I hear the lock click into place. More often than not, that sound is what brings on the nightmares of the funky images that haunt me. Weird, vague blurred pictures float in front of my eyes, wisps of old memories, but I try to force them away.

"He didn't let me leave because he wanted to talk to me," I tell Sylvie, slowly, shakily, my words strange to my own ears. It's the most I've said to her yet after all my days in her home.

"Why?" Sylvie is still holding my shoulders, staring into my eyes.

I decide part of the truth is necessary, in case Thomas is talking to Émile about what's going on. "He thinks I broke into the empty apartment."

Sylvie's forehead crinkles. "Of course you did not," she says as she pulls me into one of her warm hugs. It makes me feel worse.

"But why are you so frightened?" Sylvie murmurs into my ear. "What happened?"

I back away and shrug. After staring into my face for what seems like a very long moment, Sylvie steps away. "Okay, *chère*, let's go inside," she whispers.

Gavin is in Sylvie's apartment, standing in the entryway with his hands jammed into his pockets, shoulders hunched. His eyes meet mine as I walk in and he looks relieved.

Rage rises and spills over. How can he pretend to care after the way he's been treating me? I pull away from Sylvie and hurtle toward Gavin, slamming my shoulder into him and almost knocking him to the floor.

"Hey, what the—"

"Go away!" I scream. Furious tears flow down my face, and I don't even care. "Leave me alone, you jerk!"

I don't care that my words are weak and mangled. I don't care that Sylvie saw what I did to Gavin. I don't listen to her voice, calling after me. I don't even remember making it back to my painted, borrowed bedroom, but I huddle on the bed, hold Fat Cat tight and curse the universe.

Then, after a few seconds, I stop. I just stop. I take a deep breath and let it out in one long shudder. And I think, leaning against the wall, hugging the big cat's solid body close to me. This can work to my advantage. I'd been trying to figure out how to bring up the subject of Zander. It's cold. It's calculating. And it's what I have to do. The old lady doesn't know it, but she's just helped me out. She'll have to get used to me, because I'm going to be a permanent neighbor.

And if Thomas and his mother wanted to scare me, it didn't work. Because right now, this very moment, I swear on the graves of all the dead Impressionists that I'm going to find out what they're up to. Maybe I shouldn't be going into that empty apartment, but neither should they.

Fat Cat purrs in his sleep. I watch the shadows and try to force my brain to recapture the images I glimpsed this morning; the vague, haunting memories that have teased me since Thomas locked me inside his mother's apartment, but they slip away before they can really take shape. *What were they?*

The letter I found comes to mind. The lamp casts a dull glow about the bedroom as I fish the paper out from its hiding place under the mattress. I read it again.

Who was she, this Marguerite? Why did the man say her words were "weak"? Were they like mine? Slippery, strange, never sounding the same? And aren't there more letters? There have to be.

It's very simple to sneak back into the apartment. All I have to do is listen to make sure no one else is there. And this time, I'm prepared. I take a flashlight and push through the door in my wall.

The dusty smell surrounds me. I wish I could make it go away. It's the smell of long years silent and alone, almost like the apartment was a living thing, waiting in sadness for someone who never arrived.

As I shoot beams of light around the room I gasp in shock. Thomas and his ancient Mummy must be looking for something. How else would anyone explain the shelves, emptied of all their books, which were carelessly tossed all over the floor? Or the paintings, ripped from their frames, the canvases piled haphazardly in a corner?

When I take a step, something crunches under my feet, and I yelp and look down. A tiny figurine of a bird is now mostly powder under my Converse sneakers. And as I finger the shards, I feel like something hard and sharp is inside of me as well, something that cuts. It isn't fair. Marguerite wouldn't like this. This was *her* place, and *her* stuff. Why are they doing this? Do they think they have a right because she had "weak" words? Because she wasn't like everyone else?

I forget all about looking for more letters.

I have to save Marguerite's things.

The rolls of canvases are easy to stash up high in Ansel's closet. The paintings still in their frames fit under my bed. I like them. One is a still life, of blood red strawberries in a dish, next to a turquoise blue vase that's cracked. Another painting shows a little girl with huge, brown eyes, and in another, a group of people are sitting around a round metal table at a café that looks like the one Émile and Sylvie took me to. I like them.

It's so late. I wash dust from my hands and throw on my pajamas, finally ready to snore. Maybe tomorrow I'll start rescuing the books. I don't want Thomas or his mother to take anything else from the apartment.

They don't deserve to have anything that belonged to the woman with weak words.

Seventeen

Your mom is not happy. I mean, way not happy. She skipped work and cried all day. It's getting weird.

She'll get over it. Seriously!

She called me last night. She asked what's up with you? You're not writing to her.

Sorry, J. Don't be mad, bestie! I'm busy!

I lied. I said nothing's wrong. I'm getting tired of lying. I hate the lies and I know you, R. What's up?

Her words sink into my stomach like stones.

All morning, my little escapade last night has been heavy on my mind. Morning light helped me see reality.

What do I do with all the stuff I took? Why didn't I think about what I was doing? I want to ask Jada for help, but now I feel too guilty, because she doesn't know that I'm not coming home. When do I tell her? How?

This isn't so funny anymore.

"You are ready?" Sylvie asks me as she sweeps into the kitchen. I nod. Her long braids are gathered into a knot, held in place with a couple of clean paintbrushes. I love it. It's so *her*. I inhale the scent of paint and bread and wilting roses. My heart begins to calm. I love France. I love Sylvie and Émile. I love Nice, with its crumbling buildings and hills that sweep down to the ocean. There's so much blue here. Pale, azure sky, deep turquoise ocean, and I'm swimming in this color, drowning in it. It's not suffocating me, though. It's oxygen for my soul.

I type a quick message to Jada.

I'm sorry. I'll call you tonight.

Now is not the time to tell her, but I will. Soon. I log off. Then I pick up my paintbrush. My heart speeds up. This is the time I chose to tell Sylvie my "story" about Zander. I spent time last night looking up words, working out the best way to say it.

My art lesson begins. Sylvie says little. She demonstrates, wordlessly assists, and only occasionally murmurs suggestions. She is gentle, speaking softly, treating me as if I might break. She's done that since yesterday, when I was locked inside Mrs. Thackeray's apartment. The timing is so perfect. After a few minutes, I'm ready.

Drama time. I'm going to tell her about Zander.

"Sylvie," I say in a trembling voice, trying to work up some tears, but at the same moment, she pops up from her seat and scrambles for the door.

"Oh, la la, it's so late! I forgot! I must go, Rosie! You are all right here alone, yes?"

I blink. I don't remember anyone saying that Sylvie had to go somewhere this afternoon.

"Of course," I whisper.

"I'll be back soon," Sylvie says. And then she grabs her purse and she's gone.

The apartment is silent, except for the kitchen clock, ticking away the seconds in a leisurely manner. I deflate like a balloon that has a slow leak. For the first time since I've arrived here, I don't want to be alone. Why did Sylvie fly away like that? I get back to work. I may as well. I'll have to tell my story later.

I force my brain to focus on the canvas in front of me and paint. Hearing only the soft swish of a brush on the canvas, the muted murmurings of traffic outside and the slow *tick tick* of the clock, I breathe in the scent of paint and linseed oil, and soon I find myself wrapped in a kind of peaceful cocoon. I forget about everything for a while.

It's that lazy afternoon time when deep, warm pools of yellow sunlight form on the floor. Soon, Fat Cat joins me and curls up inside one of the sun pools, and peacefully, purringly falls asleep, a cloud of grey floating on lemon light. I'll paint him. I actually *want* to paint him. It's weird, I know. I grab a new canvas. The world disappears as I first sketch lines with a pencil, then add color. Light and dark tones create shape and add depth and dimension. I work to get the colors right. The smoky quality of the soft grey fur, the dazzling lemon of the sunlight. I don't know how much time passes, but finally, I step back to take a good look at my work.

It stinks.

Fat Cat is a big blob of flat grey, surrounded by smudges and smears of what looks like mustard. It's a hideous shade of yellow that doesn't even come close to having the lemony quality of the summer light as it moves across the wooden floor. Crushed, I let air out of my lungs in a long sigh.

Suddenly I'm aware that a gentle hand is on my arm, and I turn, startled, to look up at Sylvie. I hadn't heard her come in.

"Oh, Rosie, I've been waiting for this," she whispers. "I can read what's in your heart. I understand how you see the world." She smiles at me, her eyes alight, and I smile back, completely confused.

What kind of an artist are you? I want to say. *My painting sucks!*

We start to clean up and I try to figure out what happened. I still worry about being exposed as the fake artist that I am, but a strange thought dawns on me as I soak brushes and find lids for tubes of paint. Somehow, something altered inside me. It's like the "I want to be an artist" lie that I created to have an in with Sylvie is slowly becoming true. Bit by bit, an idea is morphing into reality, like the tiny dots of paint added to a Cezanne painting, one by one, to finally become sky and clouds and earth and people.

And now, I think, taking a breath, it's time for me to tell Sylvie my story. Unfortunately, when I return to the kitchen, Sylvie tells me she wants me to go down to the shop to help Émile. She's going out again. I can't figure out how to say what I want to. The right moment is gone, anyway. Dejected, I head downstairs.

The shop is cool inside. When I come in, Émile smiles at me in his way, calm and gentle. Clean air, full of the promise of rain, pours through the open door. I pick up a broom and start sweeping, feeling like Cinderella in rags, left behind, unable to go to the ball. I want so badly to be with Sylvie and tell her my story, but it's like fate is against me. And then, through the wide shop window I see her, hurrying by on the street, heading in the direction of the outdoor market. Where is she going?

"Can I go, Émile?" I ask suddenly, catching him by surprise. "For a walk. To Place Massena and back," I add with what I hope is a winning smile. Then, I have to repeat myself, since my words were scrambled. But I don't mind. Émile is so patient. I repeat myself, say, "Please."

Émile rewards me with an, "Ah," as he understands, and answers with his little shrug and a smile. He tells me to go, but I have to be back in one hour for dinner. "And you could buy mushrooms at the market for me," he adds, giving me some cash from the register. I give him a quick hug and fly out the door.

Sylvie is far ahead, barely visible, her braided head bobbing among crowds of tourists. I sprint after her, right through the flower market. It's early evening but the blooms are still everywhere, in pots, buckets and arranged in bouquets. The smell is fresh and sweet. The colors are so vivid. As I hurry past, I can't help thinking of all the funny names for shades of paint: cadmium yellow, alizarin crimson, cobalt blue. Sylvie would be proud. But where is she? There she is, sitting on a bench.

Most of the vendors at the food market are closing for the day, so I'm forced to momentarily abandon my quest to catch up with Sylvie. I manage to make a purchase while keeping an eyeball trained on my quarry. I point, smile, nod, and buy without saying anything. Émile hadn't given me specifics, so I choose dark brown shriveled-looking mushrooms that are surprisingly expensive. Their musty smell stays in my nose as I hurry toward Sylvie's bench. A tram passes in front of me. When it's gone, Sylvie is nowhere in sight.

With a disgusted sigh, I collapse onto the now empty bench and stare over the black and white checkerboard pavement of Place Massena. The pole guys are close by, kneeling high up on their tall platforms with their legs folded under them and their hands on their laps, patiently waiting for the sun to go down so they can shine. Crowded city sounds swirl around me. I hear trams, cars, buses, horns honking, voices that murmur, shout, and laugh. I smell the ocean and the surrounding trees and bushes. I can tell that a fresh batch of fries is being pulled from the grease vats over at McDonald's. As the scent wafts around me, I breathe in deep and almost taste them. I pull my knees up onto the bench and wrap my arms around them, closing my eyes.

I'm thinking of Nice as home, already. I know my street, my neighborhood, the naked cherub grocery store that smells like cheese and over-ripe fruit, the post office, the tiny corner shop where Sylvie buys her paint. I've planted my feet here and can already feel the tender roots growing under them, connecting me to the earth in this place of sunshine and sand, mountains and ocean. I only need to convince Émile and Sylvie to keep me. I've got to tell Sylvie my story!

Warm wind ruffles my hair, and my mood starts to rise. I smile to myself. I'm freaking over nothing. Fate was against me this afternoon, but tonight, after dinner, I'll tell Sylvie everything I've been planning to say. This will work.

Then, someone plops down onto the bench next to me, and my mood plunges to the earth.

"What's with the evil eye? I haven't even said anything yet," Gavin says in a soft voice. He's wearing bright yellow board shorts and a neon green shirt.

My eyes will explode if I have to keep staring at you.

It's what I want to say. Then, I'd tell Gavin how bad those colors clash with his hair. Then I'd tell him to get lost.

Gavin stretches out his long legs and sighs. He folds his arms behind his head and leans back, then turns and looks at me. His eyes are even darker, somehow. His expression is serious again.

I don't buy the solemn and sad-eyed concern. I stand.

"Wait, okay?" Gavin says, sitting up. "I came to see if you're all right."

"Fine," I mumble. At that moment, I catch a flash of bright pink. I've been keeping my eyes peeled for any glimpse of Sylvie, and I think I see her across the square. She's talking to someone.

I leap to my feet and stumble on the uneven cobbles, which causes me to collide with a nun carrying a big bunch of paper-wrapped cod staring at me with glassy eyes. The woman fixes her skirt and shifts the package in her arms so that it takes on the appearance of a bouquet of scaly fish, and then continues on her way without a glance in my direction. With a burning face I follow the Sister of the Dead Fish. Gavin is right behind me.

"Look," he says. He has to hurry to keep up with me. "I know you don't like me."

I keep speed-walking. A group of bicyclists pass in front of me and the woman I think is Sylvie is lost behind a blur of blue-framed bicycles.

"Okay, fine, don't talk to me. Listen," Gavin says, puffing. "I'll only say one thing. I want to ask you how you're breaking into that empty apartment."

I stop short and whirl around to face Gavin. "What?" I gasp, completely bewildered.

"So you really *are* breaking in? Wow," he says, giving me a look that's almost admiring. "You didn't admit it to that guy yesterday but I figured something was up."

Now Gavin is the one who walks away. He keeps moving, fast, so I have to sprint to follow after him, forgetting all about finding Sylvie. We hurry through the nearly vacant flower market, and once on my street, Gavin breaks into a run and his long legs easily leave me behind. I have a stitch in my side by the time I catch up with him in front of Sylvie's little shop. It's five minutes before closing, but the "*Fermé*" sign is already in place. Thank you, Émile, for closing up early.

"Why don't you invite me in?" Gavin asks with a slight grin.

"No way," I pant, which simply causes Gavin to lean against the shop door and fold his arms, so he's blocking my way. I plop down cross-legged on the sidewalk and catch my breath. Let him stand there all night. I can out-wait him if I have to. As soon as he leaves, I'll go around the corner to the main entrance and ring the bell at Sylvie's front door.

But Gavin sits down right next to me on the pavement and props his elbows on his knees.

"So why are you breaking into an empty apartment?" he asks.

"It was by accident, okay?" I say in desperation. I hate to let him hear how my words come out. I don't ever want to speak to him again, but he's forcing me to do it.

"How do you end up in a place like that by accident?" Gavin says.

"The cat went in. I had to get him out," I answer.

"So how did you and the cat get in?"

I growl in frustration and roll my eyes. I can't get away from him, and I can't avoid talking. Feeling like a total mutant, I explain to Gavin how I found the door, and followed Fat Cat into the apartment, trying to use words that aren't too long, that don't have too many of the sounds that are the hardest for me. It's exhausting.

"That's awesome! But it's just an empty apartment?" Gavin asks.

I shake my head no.

"What's in there?" Gavin asks. He leans in so close I can smell his hair gel. It's a sweet floral scent, like orchid. *Ick.* I lean away.

"Things," I say. I wonder if I can run fast enough to get around the building without him catching up.

"Like what?" Gavin leans in even more. I scoot away.

"Paintings, and nice . . ." I want to say "furniture," but know I won't get that word out clearly. "Nice things."

Gavin whistles. "Wow. Do you know who the apartment belongs to?"

I shake my head.

"It can't be the old lady, or she would have said so. Do you think she's stealing all the good stuff in there? She and that big guy?" Gavin says. His eyes gleam and he looks animated. Excited.

He stands and knocks on the shop door. I leap up and try to pull his hand away.

"Cut it out!" I yell.

"I'd like to see that apartment," Gavin says. "You know how to get in. We can do it tonight, if you invite me to dinner."

"No way!"

Gavin turns to me. I didn't mean to stand so close that I can count every freckle on his face.

He smiles. "One time, Rosemary. Just for fun," he says

in a soft voice.

The shop door opens.

"Gavin? What a surprise to see you," Émile says.

"I ran into Rosemary at the market," Gavin says. "She invited me to dinner."

Émile hesitates a second and glances at me, but then he steps back with a smile. "Of course, you're welcome to join us, Gavin. It's nice that Rosie has found a friend."

I follow Émile and my so-called friend up the back stairs. As I walk, I close my hands over the paper bag of mushrooms and squeeze, squishing it into a tiny ball.

Eighteen

Gavin eats like he hasn't seen food for days. At least he doesn't bother with conversation. I can tell he's anxious to get dinner over with and check out the apartment.

"We have a special dessert, *gâteau au fromage*, but it's not quite finished yet," Émile says. Cheesecake. What that guy said in his letter to Marguerite. I almost laugh.

"That's okay, Rosemary and I will hang out for a while," Gavin says. He grins in a conspiratorial way with me, like we've been planning this together. "She wanted to show me her room."

"*C'est vrai*?" Sylvie's incredulous face swivels in my direction, making her long, silver earrings jangle. She hasn't forgotten how I screamed at Gavin and almost knocked him off his feet.

"Uh, yeah," I say, after a second. I struggle to find a reason I would ever want to "hang out" with him, and have a sudden burst of inspiration. "I wanted to show him

Ansel's paintings." Wow. I'm so good at lying.

Hearing this, Sylvie gives us one of her wide, Mediterranean sunshine smiles and we all crowd into Ansel's bedroom. Sylvie chatters in half French, half English about her son and gestures all around.

The telltale hole-in-the-wall where the doorknob once was is now well hidden, thanks to a little creative rearranging of pillows on my bed, but the long cracks in the wall practically scream their presence. Feeling my heart skip around in my chest, I smile and nod and point along with Sylvie. Émile glows as well, but leaves soon to check the dessert. Sylvie stays and keeps chattering.

Gavin shrugs and glances at me with a rueful expression. I can tell he didn't expect the crowd.

"*Oh la la*," Sylvie exclaims. "That crack has appeared again. I should do something about it. I don't want Ansel's paintings ruined."

My smile freezes on my face.

"What did she say?" Gavin asks.

"Look, up there," Sylvie says, sparing me the need to speak. She walks over to the hidden door and traces a finger along the crack that leads up to the ceiling. "There used to be a door in that corner, a long time ago. This entire building was the home of one family. That door was shut and plastered over when they left and this building was divided into apartments."

"Who lives on the other side of the wall?" Gavin asks.

"No one, for as long as I have been here. I've heard that fifty years ago a woman lived there, but she left during the War and never returned. The apartment sits empty all this time. A shame, eh?"

Émile calls from the kitchen and Sylvie excuses herself to go help her husband. I find that I have to sit down on the bed. It was actually more of a collapse. I've been holding my breath. But she left. She didn't question me about the cracks on the wall.

"Okay, one quick look," Gavin says to me. "Come on, let's do this! I really want to see that apartment." His face is hopeful and for the first time I notice that he has dimples. He probably thinks the girls love them.

"No!" I say. "Not enough time."

At that moment, Émile calls from the kitchen, "Give us about ten minutes."

"Okay!" Gavin hollers. He turns to me. "Perfect timing," he says, grinning. "Now's our chance. Unless," he says, moving toward me, "you'd rather do something else instead." He reaches out to touch a strand of my hair, moving it away from my eyes.

Is he serious?

"Fine!" I slap his hand away. We work to ease the bed away from the wall. "One look. Fast," I add.

"Wow," Gavin says, once we're inside Marguerite's apartment. He whistles, and the thin sound fills the place. "Someone with money lived here."

I slug his arm and hiss, "Quiet! They'll hear!" I'm furious, but part of me is also thrilled that the words came out clearly. Score one for Rosemary on an otherwise crappy day.

"Ow," Gavin says with a half grin, rubbing his arm. "Tone down the violence, Rosemary."

He creeps around the room, carefully watching his step. I follow so I can keep an eye on him. I'm feeling possessive about Marguerite's home. The now familiar dust-bunny smell is almost welcoming, but my stomach ties itself into a knot at the sight that meets my eyes. The books I have yet to rescue lie in disarray on the floor, and someone attacked the furniture. The cushions were ripped open and stuffing lies scattered all over the floor. Much of the wallpaper has been torn completely away from the walls.

I survey the jumble on the floor and wonder if there are any more letters to be found. I kneel to sift through the piles, but a sudden loud squealing sound steals my breath and I'm positive my heart stops. We've been caught! But the sound comes from Marguerite's bedroom. I tiptoe through shards of a broken vase to the bedroom door.

"What are you doing?" I ask through clenched teeth. That does not help me speak clearly.

"Have you seen this? It's amazing!" Gavin grunts as he tugs on the swollen doors of the old wardrobe. "Help me, it's coming loose."

I do help, because it's *her* closet. I'd thought it was locked, but it's not. What could be inside?

We wrench the doors open and the smell of mothballs, stale fabric and the ghost of a sweet perfume drifts into our noses.

"More old clothes," Gavin says with a grimace. "I've had enough of that, but I have to say, this wardrobe is a great old piece of furniture. Probably worth a lot." He steps back and glances at me. "Don't you think?"

I don't answer, because the feel of the dress that I hold in my fingers is smooth and cool, like water. The pale aquamarine fabric must be silk. There's a dress with a thousand glittery beads sewn onto it, and shoes with pointy toes and funny little heels. In my head Marguerite dances, twirling in her glittery, silky dresses and laughing at her boyfriend, teasing him. She spoke with weak words, but it didn't matter.

I lift a carnation pink dress to my face and an even stronger whiff of the perfume I smelled on the bundle of letters drifts into my nose. And then something falls and lands with a soft "plop" at the bottom of the wardrobe. I reach down through a rainbow of fabric and find another bundle of letters tied with green ribbon.

Gavin isn't looking. He's moved away and is staring around at Marguerite's bedroom like he's looking at a museum display.

I stick the letters into my pocket and shove the wardrobe doors shut. I have to force them closed with my shoulder.

I don't succeed until Gavin joins me and helps.

"We better go now," he says. "They'll miss us if we don't hurry."

I don't argue this, and we move into the next room. Gavin pauses beside a tall, narrow bookcase, eyeing it with an approving glance. "This place is so cool. Maybe we can come back tomorrow."

"No," I blurt, glaring at him. Looking into this guy's strange, dark eyes ringed with pale lashes, anger sparks inside me and flares to life. "No way."

Gavin takes a step closer. I take a step back, nearly tripping over books and boxes on the floor.

"Why not? Is it because you don't like me? Or," he adds, lifting something in his hand. "Is it because you don't want anyone else to know you've been taking things?"

He's holding another bundle of letters. Marguerite's letters.

He shouldn't have them. They're mine.

I try to grab them. He holds on. My fingers close over his hand, the hand that holds the letters. We're standing too close.

"Why do you play these games with me?" he asks in a soft voice.

"What games?" I whisper.

His head leans in. I don't stop him.

I can't find my feet.

I can't breathe.

I. Am. Kissing. A. Boy.

A tiny part of my brain wants to laugh in triumph. Jada dared me to kiss a boy on my trip to France. But then reality snaps back into place.

Why am I doing this? For one, two horrified seconds, I'm frozen, feeling Gavin's lips, hearing him inhale, smelling the bubblegum on his breath, his flowery hair gel, feeling one hand move up my arm, the other still clasped in mine.

But I don't like him! What am I doing?

In a single unconscious movement, I place both hands onto Gavin's chest and shove, hard. He flies back and lands on his butt. Before he can react, I turn to go but stumble and grab the bookcase for support. It trembles and moves away from the wall. It falls in slow motion, each second an eternity, but finally cashes to the floor with a tremendous crash that reverberates through the apartment. Books scatter and explode and brittle pages fly, swirling like giant snowflakes in an indoor blizzard.

I freeze in horror, but Gavin hauls himself to his feet and grabs my arm. We hurtle ourselves through Marguerite's apartment and squeeze back through the hidden door and into my bedroom.

And right when we push the bed back against the wall, Émile opens my bedroom door.

"Dessert is ready," he says, looking us over with a strange expression. "And Rosie, please leave your door open when you have, uh, friends with you in the room."

Gavin's dimpled face grins at me. Émile leaves and I finally grab the letters from Gavin's hand. I'm glad he didn't drop them when he fell.

I shove both new bundles of letters under my pillow, staring at Gavin the whole time, daring him to say something.

He doesn't. But his eyes crinkle in amusement.

When we return to the kitchen, I am positive that my face is a bright Alizarin crimson.

And the cheesecake tastes like bubblegum.

Nineteen

The new bundles contain letters from different boyfriends. Each bundle is tied by a ribbon of a different color.

> Ma Chère Marguerite,
>
> How can you think that I would ever mock you? You, my darling, my beloved? When you grace the stage, the whole world adores you! I will die if you do not forgive me!
>
> I offered to find the greatest elocution coach in the world, but that does not mean that I do not love each word you say as it falls from your lips. Do not leave me alone any longer, my darling! I die by degrees each day I do not hear from you. My wife

> travels again tomorrow, say you will allow me to come to you. I beg you, my dear, please open your arms to me once more!
>
> Always,
> Georges C.

My heart leaps inside me. "Elocution." Does that mean what I think it does? I find the definition on my phone: formal or public speaking. An elocution coach isn't exactly a speech therapist, but did they even have those back then?

I read the letter again, the words in their tiny script make my eyes hurt.

This guy wrote a lot of love notes. His wife must have loved to travel. Aside from being a lying cheater, Georges thought Marguerite needed help to speak correctly. Marguerite apparently didn't like it, but what surprises me the most is what Georges says about the stage. Most of his letters are promises to meet Marguerite backstage after her performances.

Marguerite spoke with "weak words," but she was an actress.

How did she do that?

We're in the shop. June morphed into July and it's sweltering. While I look at the letter, tucked discreetly inside an old cookbook, Sylvie sits by the cash register with her bare feet up on the little wobbly table, reading the kind of book that Mom always reads. On the cover, there's a muscle-bound guy with no shirt who has a pretty girl clinging to his arm. That kind of book. Every so often,

Sylvie glances up at me from behind the pages and winks.

Why?

I heard her talk with Émile last night. His voice sounded worried. Hers was soothing, gentle, and strangely filled with mirth. Eventually, Émile sounded calmer. They laughed together.

Sylvie must think I'm in love.

In love . . . with Gavin?

I did let him kiss me.

Or did I kiss him?

I can't believe I did that!

I close the cookbook and tuck it under my arm. Then, I grab the duster and swipe at some shelves, those same little shelves full of dumb glass bottles like the one I dropped my first day here after Gavin made fun of me. My mouth is dry, and I can barely swallow. When I do, I swear I can still taste bubblegum.

I want to hurl.

"Can I go, now, Sylvie?" I ask. All I want right now is to find my toothbrush and scrub away the taste of the kiss that still lingers.

"Of course, *chère*," Sylvie says. She winks again. What's with the winking? She waves me away with a languid hand and a knowing smile.

"Go."

Half a tube of toothpaste later, I feel better.

In the bedroom, I nearly fall over Fat Cat who was parked in the middle of the floor. When he looks up at me with his glowing eyes, even he seems to be giving me that "I know what you've been doing" look that Sylvie was throwing at me in the shop. I suppress a desire to kick him.

"Shut up," I growl at him. Then I feel stupid. He can't talk and never said anything in the first place.

All of Georges's other letters still lie in a pile right on top of my bedside table. I no longer worry about hiding them, since Sylvie and Émile never come in without permission. Suddenly, I want to look for more. I want to know more about Marguerite, the actress. And after a heartbeat's hesitation, I march to the door in my wall.

With my ear pressed to the thin wood, I listen, holding my breath. I can't hear anything. Did Thomas or his Mummy hear the bookcase come crashing down last night? I know how stupid it is to keep breaking into Marguerite's home, but I find myself pulled, like there's this invisible wire wrapped around my heart. I sneak back inside.

Dust motes swim before my eyes in the late afternoon sun that slants through hazy windows. Flies buzz, droning lazily in the otherwise perfect silence. I still love it, this feeling of being so totally alone. Something that weighed me down only moments before vanishes, and I breathe in the strange sensation of being solo. No Mom. No Sylvie or Émile, as much as I love them.

No Gavin.

The downed bookcase looks pathetic, almost like a murder victim left to lie where he fell. I pick through a few of the scattered books and I find more letters immediately. They were inside a book whose pages had been cut out to form a kind of hollow apartment. They're tied with a purple ribbon.

Wow, that was easy. I shove the letters into my pocket.

I should leave, but I don't want to, not yet. I'm standing close the spot where I had my first kiss. I lift my hand to my mouth, touch my lips.

In this very room, I kissed a boy. Every little movement of his dry, chapped lips plays in my mind. The smell of his hair gel, the sound of his breathing, the toxic taste of bubblegum. Why can't I stop thinking about it?

"Because you're an idiot," I whisper into the silence.

The silence agrees with me. I swear it does.

Taking a deep breath to clear my head, I head back to Marguerite's bedroom. I want to see her dresses one more time. Then I promise myself, I'll get out of here.

The doors open more easily this time. I'm rifling through furs and gowns when heavy footsteps rumble down the inside stairs. I'm so stupid! I was so caught up in reliving The Kiss and looking for more letters that I forgot to listen for Thomas. I have no time to retreat. I've got to hide!

"I'm heading there now, Mum," Thomas's gravelly voice shouts, sounding way too close.

I sweep silk dresses aside and I'm in. My fingers find a metal bar on the inside of the wooden doors that I use to help me pull them shut. They close with a screech that makes me cringe. Then I pull mothball-smelling furs in front of me and crouch, trying not to breathe, but I end up panting because I'm so scared. I'm positive he'll hear my ragged breathing and my hammering heart. Footsteps pound into the room.

"We'll find it," Thomas shouts. "I've got some tools to open that wardrobe." Oh no. I knew it. I knew it! I suppress a gag. The stale, mothball air is getting to me. I'm positive I'm going to pass out. I gasp for air and choke on a mouthful of fur coat. Then, I hold absolutely still. He's inches away from me.

Thomas drops something heavy to the floor that lands with a metallic clang. Then, he grabs the handles of the wardrobe doors and yanks. The entire cabinet shakes. I'm surprised to find that my fingers are still gripping the interior metal bars. Somehow, miraculously, they hold tight. Thomas mumbles to himself.

The wardrobe shakes violently. Then the high-pitched whine of a drill screams in my ears and I feel the doors vibrate. My fingers lose their hold. I'll have to run for it. As soon as he gets these doors open, I'll jump out and bolt for freedom. He'll be so surprised that he'll be too slow to catch me. But as I shift around to get into a good position, my butt and my legs are numb from crouching. Besides, I'm dizzy from the hot, stale, mothball and sweet perfume air. I'll probably fall out, right smack on top of Thomas. I'm going to hurl.

The whine of the drill shuts off, and a tiny circle of light appears as one of the door handles falls to the floor with a thud. A bony finger reaches inside the hole, tugging and pulling, and I have a wild thought that I should bite that finger off. The thought only makes me feel even more like I'm about to vomit all over the dead animals and silk dresses around me. Then the wardrobe shakes once again as Thomas tugs, pulls, yanks, and wrenches, and I hear him swear, because he's hurt his finger. Miraculously, I'm still holding the door shut.

Thomas's footsteps pound away and up the stairs.

This is my chance! I push against the doors, but they don't budge. I push harder. I hear a screeching sound, but nothing moves. He'll come back and find me here! I scrabble around and brace my back against the rear of the wardrobe, and push as hard as I can with my feet. The old, rusted hinges squeal and shudder, and at an achingly slow pace, the doors start to move. Light bursts into my eyes and I fall, wrapped in silk and furs. There's a sickening sound of tearing fabric. I untangle myself as quickly as I can, grab an armful of furs to shove back inside, and I see her. It's Marguerite.

The portrait was behind the dresses, at the back of the wardrobe. It was hidden behind a panel that must have come loose when I moved around in there or got tangled and fell. The panel is now on the floor and the painting is at my feet. I drop the dresses and gingerly pick Marguerite up, forgetting that I need to get the heck out of here.

She sits on a curved chair and wears a satiny pink dress. Posed in a dramatic way, Marguerite's face is turned to the side and she smiles. Her curly brown hair isn't cut short, like that of the woman in the other painting, but is pulled up at the back of her head. Her other hand rests in her lap and her fingers are long and graceful-looking. She's everything I would imagine her to be. Beautiful, self-assured, perfect. The woman of weak words, who ruled the stage.

A door slams somewhere above my head and I

remember Thomas. I shove stuff back into the wardrobe and shut the doors, kick the fallen wood panel under the bed, grab Marguerite and run. Back in my room, I place her flat on the floor, cover her with a towel and slide her under the bed, adding her to my collection.

"Rosie?" Émile calls.

"Yes," I gasp the word out, sticking my head out the bedroom door.

"Dinner's ready. I hope you're hungry."

Not really.

Twenty

Dearest Friend,

Forgive me for addressing you in such a familiar manner. I feel certain that when you read my words, you will understand, and not consider it impertinence. Last night as I heard your clear voice from the stage, my eyes filled with bitter tears. I have always yearned for such a gift as you possess. From the time I was a child, I longed to be an actress.

Mademoiselle, I joined the waiting throng of admirers outside your dressing room after the lights dimmed. I wasn't sure why. Perhaps I only wished to see you close at hand instead of from afar. Imagine my surprise and delight when you, surrounded by men throwing flowers at your feet, caught my eye and smiled. I was not able to draw any closer because of the great press of the crowd, but I heard your voice. This is what brought even greater joy to my heart and caused me to write this letter.

I learned your secret. You, the great stage actress, speak with a stammer, as do I. What joy filled my heart! Late as the hour was, I returned home and penned this letter to you. Thank you, my dear friend, for I will always consider you such! You have made me realize that my own foolish dreams are not as foolish as I may have thought. My speech difficulty does not mean that I may not obtain what I truly desire: to recite upon the stage.

I will never forget what you have done for me this night.

Fondest regards,
Adeline Bernier

My eyes sting when I read the words "stammer." Marguerite stuttered. Before I finish the letter, my face crumples. Something way down inside me twists and tears. It fights its way out and I'm surprised by the sound that escapes my lips. It's not a wail or a sob. It's harsh and deep. A groan. No, a growl.

"Don't be stupid," I mumble to myself, gasping for air when I'm able to finally open my eyes. A tiny breeze rustles the papers I've spread out around me on the cracked tiles of my little rooftop garden. Marguerite's letters rustle in the blowing air, making soft whispering noises. It's like they've been silent too long and want to be heard. The nineteenth century fan mail is written in a few languages I recognize and many I don't.

I pace. Dirt and dry leaves crunch under my feet. I sit on the little wall at the edge of the roof and stare out over the jumble of weathered buildings that surround me. I've never noticed how run-down this place is. It's ugly. The people on the sidewalks below scurry by, unaware that I'm watching. They're all normal. I hate them. As much as I try to tell myself it doesn't matter that Marguerite wasn't like me, I still feel that pathetic hope lying all crumpled and dead inside me and it hurts.

Rosemary? Are you there?

Ignoring my mom's text, I start dropping handfuls of potting soil down onto the people who walk by. The dirt scatters and nobody notices. I try gravel. There! Bull's-eye!

Rosemary? I need to talk to you.

Ducking down out of sight, I smile as I listen to the shouts from four stories below. I'll wait a few minutes and find a new target. I toy with my phone but don't answer. I don't feel like it.

So Marguerite stuttered. I should have known. Someone who stutters can still be an actor, or a singer. Something in their brains lets them do it. When they say something on their own, they stutter. But when they pretend to be someone else, and when they sing, they're fine. They have an escape. A time when they can be normal. They're not like me. I can never speak perfectly. I don't stutter sounds or words, I slaughter them.

Someone is coming. It's time for me to leave.

When I begin to gather the letters back together, one of them catches my eye. It was written in English and is signed, "With sincere disgust." Letting the other papers fall to the tiles, I read with wide eyes.

> My Dear Mademoiselle,
>
> How is it that you can consider yourself an actress? After seeing tonight's performance, I am convinced of two things. First: it is obvious that you walk upon the stage thanks to your pretty face and form, not to your so-called ability to perform as an actress. Second: anyone who encourages you to think otherwise should be summarily examined by a licensed medical professional to determine if he is safe to remain in society, since he obviously suffers from some sort of delusion. Your diction was clumsy and confusing, rendering your performance unbearable. If you desire a life in the

> theatre, Mademoiselle, I suggest that you apply to your local theatre as a cleaning woman. Your talents are much more suited to sweeping up after those rare individuals who truly belong on the stage.
>
> With sincere disgust,
> Henry B. Billingsley

Why would Marguerite keep this letter? This man said that her "diction," which I guess means her way of talking, was clumsy and confusing. Did she stutter on the stage?

A guy in a suit and tie emerges from below, nods in my direction, picks up a watering can and meanders over to his tomatoes and peppers while keeping his cell phone glued to one ear. I gather my papers and flee downstairs. I head to my spot; this place at the end of the hall on the second floor that's like an architectural mistake. The hallway turns and leads to a wall only a few feet away from your face. I'm willing to bet there was a door there once. Anyway, the resulting space is basically a tiny room, and some kind soul left an overstuffed chair in there.

I sit and spread out the letters. Something is bothering me. I want to read the dates.

The hate letter was written in 1869. I compare the dates of all the others, stacking them in uneven piles around me. The earliest was written in 1854, and the others range all the way up to 1868. And after I've checked them all, I feel tired, deflated and sad. None of the fan letters were written after the hate mail.

Closing my eyes, I rest my head on the back of the chair. Marguerite, did you let that guy stop you from acting? Why does this thought make my heart sink inside? Minutes ago, I was almost mad at her. I was jealous, because for her, I thought the stage was a safe place where she could talk like anyone else. Now it looks like her safe place betrayed her.

When I raise my head, I see how deep the shadows are around me, so I finally gather up the letters and head to Sylvie's. I feel like my brain was thrown into a blender. My thoughts are whirled mush.

I'm almost surprised to find myself closing the apartment door behind me. Émile is watching a cooking show, engrossed and taking notes, but he turns to smile at me. Sylvie is singing in the kitchen, softly. I catch a few words. "My child, my sweet child." Her voice breaks. So does my heart.

With my back to the door, I hesitate. I am so confused. I was going to tell my story about Zander tonight. But once again, I'm reminded how much Sylvie and Émile are hurt by the unimaginable loss of their son. Is it fair for me to do this to them? To add to their sorrow, to add the burden of a terrible knowledge that's actually a lie, all so I can convince them to let me stay?

I turn at the entrance to the hallway and look back at the place that in my heart is now my home. I want to stay here, more than anything I've ever wanted in my life. I take a breath and try to imagine the words I'd say. They stick at the back of my throat, choking me. I can't do it. At least, not tonight.

With a heavy heart, I stumble to my room. Ansel's room. I pull pajamas over my head and toss my jeans to the floor. And then, I sit on the bed and stare at the floor.

I'm selfish.

I have been all along. I chose Sylvie and Émile as my host family only because they lost a son. I chose them only because Sylvie has suffered so much in her life I knew I'd find a compassionate, loving soul who would embrace me. And I hate myself for it.

I don't even really care about Marguerite! I tie her mail into a bundle and add it to the growing collection in my drawer. The pain I felt as I read the hate-filled letter was mostly for me. I wanted Marguerite to be the strong woman I'd created in my mind. I needed her to be fearless, carefree, and successful, the brilliant actress I thought she was, because of one thing. If she couldn't do it, how can I? I mean, if Marguerite couldn't ignore her weakness and still live her dream, how can boring, untalented, freakishly weird-sounding Rosemary ever live her own dreams, whatever they are?

My phone buzzes, and I pick it up. I have seventeen texts from Mom. Seventeen texts that I don't bother to read. There's one from Jada, too.

When are you going to call me, bestie?

My shoulders slump. I can't do it. Not right now.

I delete them all. I fish Marguerite's portrait from under my bed and prop it up onto a chair so I can see it. Then I curl myself into a ball and hug my knees as I look at her. I don't know how long I stare, but soon I fall asleep and dream that I'm sitting in a theatre, watching her on the stage. Her face glows and she's tall and graceful in her pink silk gown. She speaks in a clear voice, with words that flow from her like water in a brook as it speeds over stones, sure and quick.

My phone wakes me at dawn. I rub swollen eyes. I must have been crying in my sleep.

"Loser," I mumble to myself. When I switch on the lamp, Ansel's bedroom with its explosions of color takes shape before my eyes, and my heart aches inside me. I love it here. I love the narrow hallway I shuffle down and the tiny bathroom decorated with red roosters where I shower and brush my teeth. I love Sylvie's paint-spattered floors, and Émile's tattered cookbooks and gleaming copper pans that hang from the ceiling. I love my French parents, who for the first time in my life make me feel like I belong to a real family.

The front room is quiet in the early morning. From somewhere upstairs, a dog barks, and a voice quickly shushes it. Someone wearing high heels taps down the hall outside with rapid steps. The *tak tak tak* sounds grow louder and louder before they pass our door and fade away. I smile to myself, imagining it's the ghost of Marguerite. She's leaving because I discovered her secret.

My phone is beeping and shaking again. It's like the ghost of my former life, still haunting me. Inside me, something dawns bright as a sunrise. Since coming to

Nice, I've never been so terrified, and yet . . . I've never been so happy.

Maybe Marguerite wasn't as strong as I thought she was, but that doesn't matter.

I can be as strong as I need to be. Even if that means living a lie.

Taking the phone with me, I sneak out of the apartment and make my way to the fourth floor, then climb the creaking metal stairs that lead to the rooftop garden. With eyes closed to the waking world around me, I hold out my hand, balancing my phone in my sweaty palm. The morning air is cool. The phone buzzes like an overgrown insect in my hand. It's been ringing non-stop since it woke me. She's still trying to call, text, IM me. *Can I really do this, right here, right now?*

I'm tired. I'm so tired of everything. Maybe I'm selfish, but I'll do whatever I have to do to stay.

It's time to cut the final string that connects me to my old life.

Gulls call overhead. They lazily circle on currents of warm ocean air, free to go wherever they choose. They are free, and so am I. I smile.

Yes, I can do this.

I let go, and my cell drops.

I watch it as it falls. Even from four stories up I can hear the satisfying, metallic "crunch" as it lands and tiny bits scatter. No more buzzing. I smile up at the gulls, who screech loudly. I feel like they're laughing with me.

Today I declare my independence. It's time for me to speak.

Twenty-One

My hands are shaking. I will tell Sylvie about Zander this afternoon, during our scheduled art lesson, but I want things to be perfect. That's why I set up a canvas in Sylvie's studio so I can paint while she works on her books downstairs. I'm trying to recapture the images that flashed through my mind when Thomas locked me in his mother's apartment. They were my nightmare images. That's why I choose to recreate them. Thinking about them and about Thomas will put me in the right mood to tell my story. Everything has to be believable.

So I paint what first comes to me: a kid holding a teddy bear that's missing an eye and has a torn ear after years of being loved. When I step back to survey what I've done so far, it's not quite right. It's only a little kid with a toy. The tiny figure isn't nearly frightened enough to explain the vague feeling of dread that comes over me whenever I think of those nightmare visions. Not sure what to do, I dip my brush and begin to paint swirling clouds of darkness around the child. They're dark and heavy, more like a thick, oozing sludge than clouds. Suddenly, something sparks in my brain and I paint the shape of a person emerging from the sludge. It's a man, old and bent, with one hand that reaches out, almost touching the child. I step back, not breathing. It's like I can feel the fear that spills out from the painting into the room and swirls around me, like a cold fog. Why?

Émile bursts into the shop.

"Oh, la, la, it is time! Are you ready, Rosie?" he asks. His eyes sparkle as he looks at me.

"For what?" I gasp, still not quite able to breathe normally.

With a loving arm around me, Émile sweeps me from the apartment. "We have a surprise for you," he says. I'm still shaky and I've started to sweat. I take slow, deep breaths as we walk outside to Émile's car, where Sylvie waits inside.

Palm trees and the faded facades of pastel buildings whir by as I try to catch my breath. We have to stop near a frilly-looking villa lined with white pillars, because a throng of pedestrians fills the street. "They wait for a concert," Émile says with a grin. The car finally inches away and soon we pass a museum we visited before, one that looks like two buildings trying to crush the giant statue of a woman stuck between them. We pass more skinny apartment buildings that are faded and worn, like ours. Then the older buildings are replaced with different apartment complexes, bigger, more modern, cleaner. Uglier. Finally, the car starts to climb a steep hill, protesting; like a groaning old man climbing stairs.

We're in Émile and Sylvie's tiny orange "*deux-chevaux*," and the "two horse" car barely has enough room for me in the practically non-existent back seat. I squirm and try to find some leg room. Maybe my "surprise" is a trip to the cemetery, La Chance, to visit Ansel's grave. Sylvie holds a tote with bright fuchsia and yellow chrysanthemums spilling from the top. She hands me another bag that feels heavy on my lap. Bottles clink inside. Picnic lunch at La Chance? My French teacher used to talk about her visits to Paris. She would go to a big, famous cemetery filled with huge carved tombstones, and eat bread and cheese sitting next to the monument of her favorite nineteenth-century French writer. Other people do it too, drinking wine and tossing crumbs to the birds. It's a French thing, I guess, to have picnics in cemeteries so you can be around famous dead people. Or visit loved ones.

Émile hums and he and Sylvie smile at each other, and I marvel at their mood. Sylvie is little-girl giggly. Her joy is catching, and I find myself smiling a little. The fear I felt after I painted my strange memories begins to ease. *Save it for later*, I tell myself. For now, I want to make my French parents happy.

"So, where are we going?" I venture to ask.

"To see Ansel," Sylvie replies with a radiant smile she flashes at me as she turns in my direction. I smile back, shocked, but gratified. My pulse quickens and I feel a flutter in my stomach. They want to share Ansel with me.

This is good, because it practically means I'm like family to them, doesn't it? I've been trying to hint at joining the family in all my conversations with Sylvie. It's what I plan to ask after I tell my story this afternoon.

The car speeds over a bump and we all fly up to hit the roof of the tiny car that holds us inside like sardines. Sylvie laughs out loud. I join in, and then Émile, and we all laugh together. This is perfect! After we visit the grave, I'll tell my tale. Still full of sadness after being reminded of their loss, Sylvie and Émile will be ready and more than willing to welcome me into their lives. Forever.

I barely have time to register the new feeling of triumph that washes through me when the car finally crests the top of the hill and we speed down a tree-lined drive. Then we stop before tall iron gates with curving letters that spell out the name "La Chance" across the top. I look through the gates and my laughter dies. This isn't a cemetery. It's a tall, tan building with rows and rows of windows. Not a carved angel in sight or tourists throwing bread to the birds.

Sylvie hops out and opens my door, and I step out, lugging the heavy tote bag. Émile eases the car away to find a parking spot, and I follow Sylvie with dragging steps and a heart that feels like it's leaking away all of my blood. *I don't understand. I thought Ansel was dead. This isn't a cemetery.*

Inside, we pass a kind of reception area and head down a long hallway. I don't want to breathe more than I have to. The air smells like a light layer of antiseptic over a whole lot of putrid. As we move down the corridor I glance into rooms. There is an old, old man whose wispy white hair sticks up in patches on his crinkled skull. He's lying on a bed and snoring with his mouth gaping wide. In another room, a woman waves at us from her wheelchair. Her thick, gray curls cover her head like a helmet. I try not to stare at her legs, which end in puckered stumps where her knees should be. Sylvie gives her a jolly wave as she passes. The woman says something rapid, but I catch the word, *fils*, which means "son." Sylvie smiles and nods, and the legless woman smiles back.

We stop before a painted door displaying the scene of what looks like the beach close to our apartment. Wide umbrellas dot the pebbly sand and swirling turquoise water swells in the distance. I recognize Sylvie's work. Émile lopes up the corridor behind us, and catches us as Sylvie reaches to open the door, and swings it wide. She and Émile step in, and motion for me to follow.

A young man sits in a supercharged power wheelchair, watching TV. The chair is a familiar sight. Jada has one like it. The man's face is turned away, but his head is covered with dark curls and the curve of a bronze cheek is somehow familiar. Sylvie calls his name, and he turns toward us. I gasp and my tote bag crashes to the floor. The man looks toward the source of the sound and his eyes, nearly black, with long curling lashes, meet mine. He smiles. There's something pure in his face. It's a warmth full of truth, like all his thoughts are there to read, clear for anyone to see. Like he has no desire to hide who he is. I know those eyes, so like Sylvie's. I know that face, that smile that flashes so easily, so often. I've seen countless photographs. He is the painted boy on my wall.

Sylvie and Émile move closer and hover over their son, speaking softly. He responds, but I don't recognize any words.

"Rosie, meet our son, Ansel," Émile says with pride in each note of his voice. I want to say something, but when I try to breathe, to speak, it hurts. I close my mouth; nod my head, trying to read Émile's expression. Did he and Sylvie understand what I believed? That I thought their son was dead?

"Isn't he handsome, Rosie?" Sylvie says, without turning away from her son. Ansel laughs. His voice is deep, rich, but soft.

"I'd like to meet you, Rosie. Please come closer so I can see you," he whispers.

"Of course, of course," Émile says, taking my arm and leading me toward Ansel's wheelchair. "We brought you here for this very reason," he adds. "Our son is coming home, soon. We wanted him to meet our houseguest."

Houseguest. The words bore themselves into my body and settle in my chest, heavy and sharp, as I allow myself to be led closer to the man I had thought was dead.

"How do you like Nice?" Ansel asks. His words are weak and breathy, and he pauses in the middle of the short sentence, as though he's run out of air. It's then that I notice something strange attached to his neck with tape. It's a round plastic thing with a tube that connects to a whirring metal machine hung from the back of the wheelchair. It's a respirator. Ansel can't breathe without a machine.

I have to speak. Ansel is waiting. Tearing my eyes away from his throat, I answer.

"I love Nice," I stammer. I flush immediately. My words are hardly recognizable, even to my own ears. "That is, well . . . it's so full of color," I add with a rush.

"I knew," Ansel says, his liquid dark eyes never leaving mine, "that you would love it. The *Cote d'Azur* is the perfect place for an artist." He smiles once more and his face is radiant with a pure joy. "And I cannot wait to see some of your work."

Sylvie moves in to fuss over her son and arrange the collar of his shirt, and I step back.

"He's coming home," I murmur to no one in particular. Émile hears me and chuckles. When I look at him, I know shock is etched on my face.

"Yes, we were surprised as well," he tells me with a grin, misreading my expression, "but his doctors and therapists believe he is ready. At first, we wondered how we could get him up the stairs, but we think we have found a solution."

Émile turns back to his son, and I turn away. I clear my throat several times, trying not to cry. After all these weeks, sharing meals and washing dishes and laughing together, after the painting lessons and the little chats, after Sylvie's suspicions about Thomas, after all my hints, I'm still not part of the family. How could I have ever thought I would be? Even if I tell my "story," it won't matter. I feel so stupid.

"Isn't it wonderful, Rosie?" Sylvie says. She steps away from her son and twirls like a dancer, her tangerine-colored skirt billowing around her. Ansel laughs again. "My baby is coming home. I know you will love him, my Rosie! Perhaps you will both paint together some time! *C'est merveilleux*!"

I can't help it. My eyes immediately fly to where Ansel's stiff hands rest on his lap, curled like claws. I look away, ashamed. Did he see me? Did he know that I was looking at him?

Émile opens my tote bag, and we have our picnic at La Chance. Bread and fruit, chocolate, and cheese. Bubbly Orangina. I taste nothing, but chew and swallow because that's what I'm supposed to do. Ansel's useless arms remain resting in his lap. Sylvie feeds him baby-tiny bites. Émile helps his son drink, holding a straw to his lips. I try not to watch, but can't help stealing glances. Ansel can eat, but not breathe? And how is it that Sylvie said he could paint?

"A wonderful surprise, yes, Rosie?" Sylvie asks me suddenly, with twinkling eyes. She looks away before she sees my slight nod. And Émile fusses with something on Ansel's chair, and then he places the bright chrysanthemums in a vase beside the bed, and Sylvie continues to feed her son, chattering and smiling. I feel like an object in a still-life painting. There really isn't any room for me in the family I thought I'd found for myself. I'm the houseguest, like Sylvie said. And suddenly, the tears I'd been trying to keep hidden course down my cheeks.

"*Mais, Rosie, qu'est-ce que tu as*?" Ansel says. "What's wrong?"

I gulp and swipe at my wet cheeks, turning my face away. I feel the gentle pressure of Émile's hand on my shoulder. Hot tears fall even faster. Kind, soft-spoken Émile. He is who I had chosen to be my father. And part of me still wants to turn to him and feel his arms around me, but I don't. The painting I'd started this afternoon comes suddenly to my mind, sharp and clear. I'm the figure from my painting, surrounded by the menacing, black sludge. I imagine that dark cloud engulfing me, invading my body. I feel it pouring inside, poisonous, acidic, eating away at everything inside. I'm drowning. I'm dissolving. I am nothing.

I wrench myself away from Émile's gentle hand.

"How will *you* paint?" I blurt, gesturing in Ansel's direction. Ansel turns his head toward me, his dark, beautiful eyes meet mine, and I read the hurt that fills them. It's etched onto his face.

Sylvie's head whips around toward me, and she opens her mouth to speak, but I can't stop the words that keep falling from my mouth.

"How are you going to paint? You can't even hold a paintbrush!" The words slur as they leave my lips. I turn.

Doorways blur by me as I run back down the corridor. The gray-haired woman is still in her wheelchair in the hall. She calls out something as I race by. I hear Émile's voice shout, but I don't stop. Once I get to the parking lot, I'm stuck. I don't know the way back home, and I have no money for a bus. People are looking at me, so I slow to a trot and look for Émile's two-horse car.

Why did I say those horrible things? Rosemary, the girl

who is always so afraid to speak, spews poison words when she opens her mouth. Maybe darkness is all that I have left. I feel the cloud of sludge churning inside me, burning like acid. I feel it in every cell of my body. I'm supposed to be happy right now for someone else. Someone I thought dead is actually alive. But the sludge took over, and it won't let me to feel anything but darkness.

Émile's orange *deux-chevaux* is parked ahead, with the wheels halfway up on the curb. I try the doors, find them unlocked, and throw myself onto the backseat.

After what feels like a year of slow, crawling, empty moments, Émile and Sylvie come outside. They get in, the engine starts, and we drive back to their apartment. No one speaks. I don't care. They're not my family. They don't need me like I thought they did. Ansel isn't dead.

Twenty-Two

"I'd like you to finish the work you started yesterday," Sylvie murmurs, not quite meeting my gaze. "I'll be back later." And with that, she's gone, leaving only a hint of her lemon scent in the air.

I haven't even seen Émile once this morning. Hazy sunlight from the windows hurts my tired eyes. The nightmares danced in my head for so, so long last night.

I lift my brush and try to work on the picture I'd begun yesterday, the portrait of the strange little girl. It should be easy. I only need to paint my bad dreams, but it's impossible. I can't concentrate. I feel more and more like my oxygen was cut off. I destroyed my phone, so Mom can't contact me. By now, she and Zander must know that something is up. But that hardly matters. There's no way they'll find me.

The problem is, what do I do when the summer ends and Ansel comes home? I have nowhere to go. I have no one. My plan lies in a million pieces on the cool tiles of a hospital floor. I never saw this coming.

"It's all your fault, Ro," I whisper out loud. I was blind to how stupid my plan really was. Blame it on how badly I wanted it to work. I thought Sylvie was the perfect choice. She was the one who would most likely believe me and take me in. But I didn't understand what she said in her blog about Ansel. She said she "lost" him. She never said he died.

Minutes go by and the soft hum of the refrigerator is like a background lullaby, soothing me a tiny bit. After a while, I lift my brush, dip it in some paint, and try to do that "stream of consciousness" thing Sylvie once told me about, where you start painting with random colors and see what happens. Long strokes create dark hair pulled into pigtails tied with bows. The child I'm painting is a girl wearing a yellow sundress and sandals. She has wide, frightened eyes and a small nose, but no mouth, because she has no voice.

And my confusion melts away and I remember.

The girl in the painting is lost, and something about the way she stands, clutching the ragged teddy bear, shows her fear. She can't find her mother. She walked away in the store, and it was such a big store. She can't ask for help, because no one understands what she says.

It all plays in my mind. Finally, the nightmare images make sense. The dress, the sofa, the peanut butter.

As if I'm watching a video on a tiny screen in front of me, I watch as the other figure on the canvas, the old man, reaches out to the girl. He's kind but confused. He takes the girl's hand. He says that he will help her. He takes her to his home and gives her watery soup and canned peaches, and she sleeps on his torn sofa, and wakes and cries because she doesn't know where she is. The old man sings to her, and calls her a funny name. "Don't cry, Jenny-girl," he says. She tries to tell him her real name, but she can't. She asks for her mother, but he covers her with a blanket and she goes back to sleep.

As everything comes into focus, I paint all my nightmare images on the canvas. A red dress with puffed sleeves. Scuffed black shoes, stretched out by someone else's toes. Squares of stale crackers, smeared with peanut butter. An old black and white TV set that shows fuzzy-pictured cartoons. And a calendar, with four days marked in red. The girl stays with the kind, confused man for four days. She eats his food and wears the ragged red dress with puffed sleeves and the black shoes, and watches fuzzy no-color cartoons. The man braids her hair and calls her Jenny, and she cries, but he pats her head and sings songs about pretty horses and twinkling stars. And on the fourth day the doorbell rings, and it's a woman named Jennifer, the man's grown-up Jenny. Her eyes grow wide and she says, "Daddy, who is that little girl?" and she calls the police.

The colors on the canvas swirl together before my eyes, but I swipe the tears away because I'm not done. I turn the brush around and use the handle to gouge lines into the canvas. The lines form letters that slash across the girl: Shreveport.

Shreveport is where Mom grew up and Grandma used

to live. Where I was lost in the big store. I stayed lost for four days. It was June. The air was heavy and wet, and the cicadas sang me to sleep at night as I slept on that worn sofa. When the police called Mom and she came to get me, she held me and cried and cried, and promised she'd never leave me alone again. And she never, ever did. Not until I tricked her into letting me come here.

My paintbrush drops to the floor. Now that I remember what happened, I can't stop the memories. They're vivid, like images in fresh paint. They crash through my head. I close my eyes and see the door close and hear the lock click into place. I taste the peaches, the peanut butter, and feel gentle, trembling hands braid my hair. I see the faces of kids at school, staring when I talk, some of them laughing, pointing. As a child, I'd flee to the safety of my mother's arms. But I'm no longer a child.

For so many years, my world was my bedroom, locked from the outside. My world was the inside of Mom's car, to school and back, one gray classroom like another. It was the speech clinic. It was lunch in Mom's office. My hair in little-girl bows. "Matching Shirt Mondays," where Mom and I were "twins." Hanging out with Jada, my one and only friend, but only if Mom was there. No wonder when I arrived in France, I felt as if the scenery had changed from black and white to bright, glorious color.

More memories of the past few weeks tumble around in my head. Gavin's strange, hypnotic eyes stare at me. His words are mean and mocking, but he kisses me. Jada's barking laugh and Mom's lectures ring in my ears. Thomas grabs my long braid and my scalp throbs. Mrs. Thackeray groans as she shuffles up the stairs. The smells of dust and mothballs and sweet perfume fill my nose. Smooth silk brushes my fingertips. And a woman whose eyes gleam sends me a direct challenge. "Come on, Rosemary. You can do it. Bring it," she says. It's Marguerite.

I head to the bedroom and pull Marguerite's portrait out from under the bed. She's perfect. Confident. Happy.

"But you gave up, too," I whisper to her picture. "Didn't you?"

If only she could tell me what happened.

Hugging the painting to myself, I make a decision. I hate to think that Marguerite gave up, so I won't believe it. And wherever I end up, I'm going to keep something of her with me, always. No matter what happens. Wherever I go, I'm taking this painting.

The doorbell rings. Maybe it's Émile, who often forgets his key. I shuffle to the front room and don't even think about what I've got in my hands until I open the door.

"Good afternoon," Mrs. Thackeray says. She sees the painting and gasps, holding her shriveled hands to her mouth.

"Where did you get that?" she says, reaching toward me. I back up, but not fast enough. Her fingernails scrape my skin as she tears Marguerite from my hands.

"Wait," I splutter in a terrified squeak, not even sure of what I'm going to say.

"This was my grandmother," Mrs. Thackeray says.

Her grandmother? I stumble backward as Mrs. Thackeray comes inside, taking her tiny old-lady steps.

She clutches the painting to her.

"Where is Sylvie?" she croaks.

I shrug weakly, feeling the room twirl around me. Mrs. Thackeray heads to the kitchen.

"I shall wait here. Find her," she barks.

I shake my head no. My heart is breaking at the loss of the painting I'd claimed as my own moments ago.

"Well?" Mrs. Thackeray says, shooting me a glare full of acid. I remain where I am. I don't want to let the painting out of sight. *It's mine*, I want to say. The clock on the wall, a big silver metal thing that is shaped like a coffee pot, ticks loudly, in time with my hammering heart.

"Who is it?" Sylvie calls from the front hall. She sweeps in and gasps. I follow her gaze. She's looking at my painting on its easel. "Oh, Rosie! Why, it's . . . eh . . ." She studies it for a moment. Something in her face softens, shifts . . . she shakes herself and turns to the old woman. "Excuse me for not greeting you, Mrs. Thackeray. I . . . Well . . ." and Sylvie flutters her hands for a moment, and I stare. Sylvie is never at a loss for words.

Then Sylvie flies across the kitchen and grabs my shoulders, stares into my face. What is she looking for? She suddenly hugs me, holding so tight I can hardly breathe.

"It's all right," she whispers. I feel a tiny burst of hope. I'm about to ask her what she means by that, but then she steps away and faces the old woman who sits, watching us.

"Hello, Mrs. Thackeray," she says with a soft smile.

"Rosemary was about to tell me where she found this painting," Mrs. Thackeray says, ignoring the polite greeting and holding up the portrait.

I grope for words, feeling the gaze of two pairs of eyes. The accusation in Mrs. Thackeray's face is terrifying. Sylvie exclaims over the portrait and moves closer to examine it.

"It was in the shed," I say, desperate. My lie knifes me in the gut. Lying really doesn't get any easier.

Sylvie's face is incredulous. "The shed on the roof?" she asks, as she places a kettle on the stove and fetches cups from the cupboard.

"Yes," I answer, completely miserable.

Mrs. Thackeray stares at me with a strange, pinched expression that does nothing to improve her already shriveled appearance.

"I'd like you all to come for dinner," she says, suddenly, strangely, dropping her former inquiry. "Tonight. It's rather short notice, but I do hope you can come." Her words are directed at Sylvie, but her eyes never leave mine.

"That would be lovely, but we already have plans. Tomorrow we are having a little party. Would you like to join us, perhaps?" Sylvie says. She places a cup on the table in front of Mrs. Thackeray.

"Yes, thank you. I would like that very much," the old woman says. "Please, sit, both of you. You're not entertaining the Queen. I'm simply your neighbor."

Sylvie laughs at this. To my horror, I find myself guided to a chair right next to the old lady. I plop down and stare at the window, where a fly buzzes, caught between glass and wire screen. Out of the corner of my eye, I see Mrs. T. smile and pick up her tea. Sylvie turns her back to open a cupboard, and as she does, the old lady leans toward me.

"Tommy and I have been wondering how we might retrieve what's missing from the apartment," she murmurs in my ear.

Straightening, she sips her tea and says in a normal voice, "Delicious, Sylvie. Do I detect a hint of hibiscus?"

Sylvie nods, smiles, and sets bread on the table, and again she turns away, this time to retrieve jam from the fridge. Mrs. Thackeray leans over once more.

"The police don't need to be involved if you return everything by tomorrow before the party," she murmurs in my ear. She straightens and sips her tea as Sylvie returns to the table and I digest the old bat's threats. I mumble something unintelligible about being tired, shove back my chair and vanish into the bedroom. I stand with my back braced against the door, fighting the urge to find something to throw.

What was she telling me? Marguerite was her grandmother. Does that mean that Mrs. Thackeray owns the all the lovely paintings, sculptures and books? The dresses? It isn't fair.

Working as quietly as I can, I stuff the rolled canvases into my suitcase and cover larger framed pieces with blankets. I don't care if she's the rightful owner. I'm not giving this stuff back to the old lady. Then, I stand and put my ear to the door. I'll wait until the hag is gone. Once she leaves, I need to borrow Sylvie's phone. I pray that Jada can help me one more time. I've got to find a new family.

Twenty-Three

The old lady finally leaves, taking *my* painting with her. Sylvie quietly knocks, but I don't open the door. As much as I'd like to talk to her and know what she meant when she said everything was all right, there's something else I have to do first. So, stretched out on the bed, I don't open my eyes when Sylvie peeks inside. She sighs and eases the door shut.

Once the apartment is empty, I grab Sylvie's cell and shove it into my pocket, then smuggle heavy loads down the stairs, cursing the fact that this building doesn't have an elevator. Once everything is on the ground floor, I lug it with me and sneak out the back way, through an alley that reeks of fish.

Once I'm away from Sylvie's street, I'm safe in the anonymity of a thriving tourist town. I'm grateful that Nice is crowded and busy all day long, full of people who ignore me. I'd counted on that. The narrow lanes are filled with shoppers who carry bright mesh bags spilling over with bread, vegetable leaves or antique shop treasures, and students or tourists with massive backpacks slung over aching shoulders. No one pays any attention to the teenage girl struggling along with a bulging suitcase, as well as a massive bundle that teeters atop a child's wooden wagon.

I was counting on the key to be there, and it still is. I open the door and bring everything inside. Soon, I'm done. The heavy, green door of the Church of the Seven Wizards squeals loudly as I pull it closed. The lock makes a satisfying *clunk* as I turn the key. Not all locks are bad. I smile grimly to myself. Then, I pocket the key. Someone *will* likely find all this sooner or later, but at least it won't be the old woman. I try to imagine the scene as someone, wizard or landlord, makes their startling discovery. I think I created a nice display inside the Wizards' one-room church. The biggest painting, one almost as tall as I am, of a blue-faced acrobat with a contorted body, is propped up on the card table, which now sits, altar-like, against the far wall. I set Marguerite's crystal candelabras on either side of the painting. Every inch of floor space is covered with colorful canvas. I even hung a few on the walls, where old, bent nails still cling to bare plaster.

"Goodbye," I whisper out loud to the closed green door. A nice touch of melodrama, I thought. Mrs. Thackeray can call the police, but I don't know anything. I'm nothing more than a young girl who can't speak correctly, here for the summer to study art. They can look all they want in Sylvie and Émile's apartment, but they'll never find anything.

I make it to the nearby bus stop and collapse onto the bench, where I pull out Sylvie's borrowed phone.

> Jada, are you there? Please, please, please answer me!

Sylvie said things were "all right," whatever she meant by that, but Ansel is still coming home, which means I am homeless when summer ends.

I have to talk to my best friend. I need her help.

The phone suddenly rings in my hand, startling me. Jada! She's calling, instead of IMing me back? Why, when it's so hard for her to talk on the phone?

"Girlfriend!" Jada says, as soon as I pick up. I hear her laughter in the background, so loud it practically drowns out her stiff, robotic voice.

"Jada, I have to talk to you," I say, but she wasn't done talking to me.

"Mitch and I engaged!"

She only leaves out words when she's excited. "What?" I splutter.

I hear Jada's labored breathing as she prepares her next sentence. I usually like the wait, because I can think about what I'm going to say next, and how I'll say it. Now, the waiting is like watching ice melt at thirty below. My raw nerves scream and I can't sit any longer. Instead, I pace back and forth in front of the bus stop. A large woman with several chins stares at me.

Ignoring her, I count seconds that tick on the large,

ornate clock atop a metal post at the corner of the street. Twenty-two seconds pass.

"I want you to be my maid of honor," Jada finally says.

"What?" I blurt, breathing hard, like I've been running. I don't know how many more surprises I can digest today. "Do your parents know?" I squeak.

Forty-two seconds tick by, achingly slow.

"Yes. I have to wait until I'm eighteen. Mom said."

I'm shocked. Not that Jada's Mom said to wait until she was "legal," but that she said yes at all. Because Jada will never be able to live on her own. Neither will Mitch. They think they're going to get married?

"Uh, okay, Jada. I mean, congratulations," I finally say. "I'm happy for you, seriously. But please, listen, okay? I need help!" I plead.

Six seconds pass.

"What?" she answers. Finally, she's listening.

"I wasn't going to come home," I whisper. There. I said it. It was hard to push the sounds out, but I did. Clearing my throat, I raise my voice and pour out the whole story, sounds vomiting out of my mouth and mixing together into what would be nothing more than a stream of nonsense syllables to anyone but Jada. She always understands me. So, I tell her everything, turning my back on the woman with the bulging chins whose dark eyes continue to stare with open curiosity.

I tell Jada about the paintings, and Mrs. Thackeray, trying as hard as I can to speak clearly. I tell her about Ansel still being alive. I even tell about Gavin and the kiss as an afterthought. I'm dying for *someone* to know. Jada listens, gasps once in a while, but most often barks out her harsh laughter. How can she think this is funny?

"Jada?!"

She doesn't answer for another forty-three seconds. I pace even more, trip over someone's feet. The bus arrives; everyone else gets on, the driver waits, staring at me. Finally, I notice his quizzical expression, with bushy eyebrows almost touching his hairline, and wave him on. He makes that typical French grimace combined with a shrug that means, "Whatever," and closes the bus doors.

Jada finally talks. "I don't laugh at you. Mitch is here. He's so funny!"

My head is about to explode.

"Jada, how could you? You didn't even listen! What do I do?" I shriek into the phone. "Ansel's coming back home, so I have nowhere to go when summer is over. I need you to help me find a new exchange program, fast. Please! Help me!"

The answer comes in a few seconds.

"What?" Jada asks. I don't hear any laughter this time.

"Didn't you hear what I said? I'm not going back to Idaho! I can't go back to Mom, Jada! I can't . . ." I sob. "It would be like going back to prison!"

I take a trembling breath and try to fight the tears, but they won't stop.

Five seconds later, Jada responds.

"Prison?" she asks.

I try to control my tears and make my words come out slowly. "It's true, Jada. I've never been anywhere without my Mom since, well, since Shreveport. I mean, since I was four! I'm never alone. Ever."

This pause has to be the longest, but I don't count the seconds. My eyes are too blurred with tears to see anything.

"You're coming back in August. Right?" Jada finally asks. Now, she's starting to get it. She finally gets that I wasn't only coming here for the summer. I gulp.

"I was never planning to go back to Idaho, Jada. I wanted to stay here. Now, I can't stay in Nice, but if you help me, maybe somewhere else in France . . ." My words trail off.

I hear background noise again, but this time it's not laughter. Jada is mad. Really, really mad, because she's squealing, grunting and yelling, and her head is thrashing around like it does when she's agitated.

"You can't stay there!" she finally says.

"I thought there was a way I could do it, Jada! I thought that Sylvie and Émile didn't have Ansel anymore, so they had room for someone else. And I knew they would feel sorry for me . . . don't you get it?" I say, sobbing. Saying it out loud makes a cold lump of squirming embarrassment form in my stomach, because hearing my voice say the words makes it totally obvious to me how crazy the plan was from the beginning.

"It won't work, now, because Ansel is coming home. And I said bad things and hurt Sylvie, and I got mixed up with that old lady and took stuff from that apartment. I know it was crazy! Now I have to find another place to go! Please, help me, Jada!" I add, gulping and gasping for breath. Crazy plan or not, I'm here now, and desperate not to go home.

"I helped you lie to go to France! I helped you steal! I'm your best friend but you lied to me, too!" Jada says.

"I *am* your best friend, but I couldn't tell you. I was afraid you'd think I was crazy." I hear her grunt as she works on her response. Ten seconds go by.

"Crazy and stupid."

My tears stop. Everything stops. No breath is in my lungs. The black sludge is still inside. I feel it spreading from somewhere around my heart to the rest of my body. My best friend, who always stands up for me when no one else does, who tells me I can do anything, who tells me to "bring it," called me crazy. And stupid. Jada can't even talk without a computer, or move without a wheelchair. Neither can Mitch. They think they're getting married. And she thinks *I'm* crazy and stupid?

Once again, my mouth moves before I think about what to say. Maybe it's my . . . apraxia. There. I allowed my brain to think it, the word I hate so much. Maybe it's the sludge inside. Sounds plummet from my lips, quick and garbled, but I know Jada will understand me.

"Crazy and stupid? You know what's crazy and stupid, Jada? That you and Mitch think you can get married! That's a joke and you know it! Where are you going to live? At Cascade Hills, with Mitch? So the nurses can feed you and change you at the same time? That's romantic."

Jada squeals as I struggle for breath, feeling my heart drum with anger. Jada's mom probably told her "yes" to get her off her case. But Jada will never live by herself. She can't walk. She can't talk without her computer; she can't even eat. Someone has to feed her through a tube in her stomach. Someone has to bathe her, change her clothes and do her hair. Someone has to change her diapers.

She's a lot like Ansel.

Ansel. The name carves itself into my mind, and once again, I see brown-black eyes that fill with pain at the sound of my words. What would I read in Jada's eyes if I were standing before her now? How could I have spoken those cruel words? She's my best friend. We laugh together, get crushes together, and cry together. She is the one person who always defended me and has never, ever mocked my mushy words. Why *can't* she and Mitch get married? Why *shouldn't* they? Why do I keep saying such awful things to everyone around me, even the people I love the most? My words were true, but they're horrible.

"J," I start to say, but I hear a click and my throat starts to close.

Jada hung up.

Twenty-Four

I sleep so late it's no longer morning. Sylvie must have hit the flower markets, because the kitchen is smothered in plant life by the time I wander in, looking for food. Clouds of pink, crimson, blue, lavender, yellow, and green cover every surface. I smell roses, lilacs, carnations, and other flowers I don't recognize. Underneath it all is the smell of roast chicken and lots of garlic.

Wrinkling my nose, I grab a pear and sink into the nearest chair. The fruit is tasteless so I give up on it after a few bites and sit, staring at a smattering of crumbs on the table, wondering where I'll go when autumn comes. During the night I researched student exchange programs. One in Milan sounds promising. It's for English speakers, so I don't even need to speak Italian. I've already done the online application but need to fake some actual paper forms. I'll use the same credit card I'd applied for in Zander's name, like I did to pay for this program in

Nice. But won't that make it too easy to trace me? I don't know. My head hurts. Maybe I'll go back to bed. Say I'm sick. Rubbing my eyes, I head back to what used to be my bedroom.

My things are piled outside the door. Clothes are in one pile; shoes are lined up along the baseboards. Two of my stupid "happy tree" paintings lean against the wall. I stop, gasp, and feel like my world is about to implode.

Not yet. I don't have anywhere else to go!

"Oh, Rosie, here you are," Émile says, emerging from Ansel's room. "I was cleaning out Ansel's closet, trying to find his old books. I'd wondered where your suitcase was. What did you do with it?"

Blinking in shock, I try to answer. "I, um, well—" Too late, I finally remember I'd left it down in the shop after returning from the Wizard's Church.

Émile regards me for a moment with a thoughtful expression, looking a little sad. Finally, he shrugs.

"No matter, you can help me put your things back. Then we must prepare for our dinner tonight."

Several times I find myself simply staring at the object I'm trying to put away. My mind won't focus on anything. We finally finish and head to the kitchen.

"Who is coming for dinner?" I manage to ask. It's silly, almost. I know who's coming, but I want to hear it again.

"Our friends, Phil and Valerie, and their son. I'm sure you'll enjoy seeing them again," Émile says with a slight grin. I grimace in return. At least Gavin won't try to kiss me in front of the group. I hope.

"Also," Émile adds, looking up from the roast chicken

he was basting, "Ansel will be here. This dinner is in his honor. To celebrate his homecoming."

"Oh," I say, trying but failing to smile. Instead I turn away and finger the petals of a pale pink rose. "That's nice."

"That's why we'll eat in the shop tonight. Sylvie is they're making everything ready for us. You can help me bring down some chairs." Émile turns back to his chicken.

So we're having a party. I shred petals and drop them onto the counter. A party with everyone I don't want to see.

It's time to say goodbye. I tried, but my plan didn't work.

It kind of feels like my heart melted and is sloshing around in my shoes. I follow Émile and help him carry down metal folding chairs to Sylvie's little shop. We move shelves, clear space in the middle of the floor, set up a long folding table. Sylvie is busy in the back rooms, and doesn't emerge. I don't mind. I don't speak, except to ask when the guests will arrive. I'm told I have about an hour.

Once chairs and table are in place, I say I need to shower to get ready for the party. I grab my suitcase from where I'd stashed it, behind the rack of bright skirts, and let it bump against each step as I return to the upper floor.

Ansel's bedroom feels different. It even *looks* different somehow. It's cold and sterile. The colors are no longer bright. It's the room of a stranger, a place where I don't belong. I pack quickly and quietly. I don't yet have a new family, but at least I have a temporary sanctuary until I can find one. I pat the key to the Wizards' church in my pocket to be sure it's there. And then I turn to say goodbye to the room I love.

Fat Cat grunts at my feet, wanting me to let him out. I gather the purring feline in my arms and bury my face in his soft fur.

"I'll miss you, cat."

I ease the door closed behind me and pull the suitcase down the hall. I'll have to borrow Sylvie's phone again until I can get my own. I'll send it back to her as soon as I can. The kitchen is empty, so I grab the phone, shove it into my pocket and stuff the charger into my suitcase. I look around the kitchen once more, wanting to remember, but it hurts too much. Blinking, I whirl around and rush to the front room, wanting to escape quickly before anyone comes back upstairs.

I'm too late.

Gavin and his parents are here in the front room, sitting on the little couch. I yelp when I see them. Valerie wears a sweet grin, Phil fake-smiles in my direction, and Gavin just stares at me with his weird eyes. My face bursts into flames. Then, someone clears her throat, and I turn toward Mrs. Thackeray. She's actually holding Marguerite's portrait, the ancient witch! Why did she bring it with her? To gloat? The old lady nods a greeting at me with a smug smirk on her face. I have the sudden urge to grab Marguerite from her and run.

Émile rushes in and places a tray of drinks onto the coffee table. "Rosie, can you help?" he asks. "Our guests are a bit early. Sylvie has already left to pick up Ansel." And with that, he hurries again into the kitchen, not noticing my suitcase. The doorbell rings. "Please get that," Émile calls from the kitchen.

Everyone turns their eyes to me. Gavin stares at my suitcase. Phil looks perplexed as usual, Valerie's smile starts to slip a bit, and Mrs. Thackeray pins me in her gaze like a cobra. Forget this. Forget them. I'm still leaving. Grabbing the handle of my suitcase, I go to answer the door.

I'm drowning. A whirlwind, a hurricane, a tsunami crash into me and engulf me all at once. I feel all the oxygen leave my body. It's *her*. She found me.

"Rosemary! Oh, it's really you! How could you do this to me?" Mom shrieks, while her long arms grab me and I'm caught. She holds on tight. Her voice breaks. I feel her sobbing against me. She's crying, and has been for a while, from the looks of her puffy eyes and runny makeup. How did she find me?

Zander is here, too. He stands behind Mom, his tall frame wobbly and ill at ease, as usual, his blond hair tangled and dangling down over his forehead. His eyes are bloodshot and baggy and his face is gray. Mom tries to squeeze every last molecule of air out of my lungs.

"Who is it?" Sylvie calls from hallway outside the apartment. She hurries up, and then a wondering expression spreads over her face. "Your mother, Rosie?" she asks, dark eyes wide. She doesn't wait for an answer, but calls, "Émile, come, come, look who's here!" She gestures for Mom and Zander to enter and shoos them inside, while Émile comes in, looking suddenly even more harried and distressed.

The tiny front room is full of people all talking at once. Mom keeps one arm around me, holding tight to my shoulder. "Well, Rosemary," she says, sniffing and practically digging her nails into my skin, "you haven't said anything! I'm sure you're surprised to see us." Her ragged voice is hard-edged, laced with fury. She throws a significant look at Zander, who gives a slight shake of his head. "Get your things. You and I are going to have a nice, *long* talk."

She dissolves into tears again. Sylvie hands her a tissue, invites her and Zander to join us for dinner. Zander accepts. He tells Mom we can wait a bit and I can leave after dinner so I can say my goodbyes. I still don't think anyone has noticed my suitcase, now sitting forlorn and forgotten by the front door.

Ansel is waiting downstairs. Sylvie shoos us all down the hall and to the back staircase, and we all squeeze through the door and troop down in one big, noisy group.

They found me. How? Then, as I squirm under my mother's hand, still gripping my shoulder, I feel like a bucket of ice water was dumped over my head. Jada. She must have told her.

Everyone spills into the shop and keeps talking. Ansel is there at the head of the table, smiling, laughing, while his machine whirs and breathes for him. Sylvie and Émile introduce everyone. I pull away from Mom and go to sit at the little chair behind the cash register, partly hidden from the group. Mom lets me go but keeps her red eyes fixed on me. Zander wanders and stares at paintings on the wall. Chatter whirls around me for two, three long, long, long minutes. Sylvie's voice rises above the others.

"You mean you did not know that Rosie was in France? *Mais, c'est impossible!*"

Émile's voice rumbles after Sylvie's, softer, calmer. Trying to soothe. Oh, Émile! My eyes fill with angry tears. They spill down my face, and I don't bother to wipe them away.

I only wanted to get away from my mother. I wanted to so badly that I lied, I stole, and I went to another country! I did everything I could to carve myself a place within this new family. Things obviously didn't go like I'd planned, but at least I was on my own.

Then, Mom showed up. She found me because my best friend betrayed me. My only friend . . . wait! I think of someone with auburn hair and an easy smile. Nicole! She told me to visit her in London. I'll send her a text. If I have her address, I can figure out how to get there. Maybe I can find a way to slip out while everyone is talking.

Hey, it's Rosemary. Can U send me your address? I'm on my way to London.

I hit send and bite my lip while I swipe away tears. Voices rise and fall like waves lapping against the pebble-strewn beaches of Nice while I stare at the phone, waiting, praying. It beeps. I read the words that appear.

Who is this???

Doesn't she have Sylvie's number? Maybe she was just being polite. *She's a supermodel, Ro. She doesn't actually want to be your friend.*

The voices die away. When I peer around the cash register, Gavin's bright copper head swivels in my direction. He holds up a small white card in his hand with an expression of amusement on his face. It's one of Mom's "Childhood Apraxia of Speech" info cards. She likes to hand them out. Valerie has one, too. She says, "Ah," as she reads it.

Hashtag humiliated times infinity. I'll go to London anyway. I hear they have work for sideshow freaks.

Mrs. Thackeray speaks.

"Please listen, all of you. I have something very important to say," she announces. "You probably do not know that I am the owner of this building." Sylvie and Émile gasp. Ansel's eyes widen. The corners of the old lady's mouth curve upward in a tiny smile.

I loathe her.

"It once belonged to my grandmother, a famous actress whose portrait I hold in my hands." She pauses and gazes around the room, like we're all supposed to applaud, or something. "This building is mine. I plan to hand the ownership over to my son Thomas when I return to England next month." Mrs. Thackeray clears her throat, a wet, gravelly sound that turns my stomach. Then, she looks around at everyone. The shop is silent, except for a couple of coughs and a long wheezing breath from Gavin, who must have caught a cold.

"You needn't worry," Mrs. Thackeray continues. "Tommy will take good care of things. However," she pauses to dab her face again, "his plans do change things, a bit."

"Change things? How?" Sylvie says in a trembling voice.

"You see, we looked at my grandmother's records, and these flats were not supposed to be two-level homes. Only single-level flats. Tenants who are using two floors will have their rent adjusted accordingly. If they do not wish to pay more, they will need to move out of the extra rooms they have been using."

"But, we have a contract," Émile says. His face is so distressed, my heart breaks for him.

"All contracts were intended for single-level flats," Mrs. Thackeray repeats, speaking slowly, condescendingly, as if speaking to a small child. She sits primly in her chair with her stupid poufy hat on her head, and I hate her more than ever.

"Forgive me. We really shouldn't discuss business at dinner," Mrs. Thackeray says. "I only brought this up because I know Rosemary is quite interested in my grandmother's flat. The empty one next to yours, you know. She's been sneaking in there quite often, I believe. And there is a matter of grave concern. She must return all the stolen property or I will press charges today." She looks at me with a gleam of triumph in her faded eyes.

All heads swivel in my direction.

Gavin hurries over to me and presses a piece of paper into my hand, keeping his back to the group so they can't see what he's doing. He doesn't say anything at first, because he's coughing again, but finally he chokes out a harsh whisper. "Just read it, okay?" He moves away and goes off to hack by himself in a corner.

"What does she mean, Rosemary?" Mom asks, practically shouting to be heard over all the other voices that talk at once.

I open my mouth, but no words come out. There is nothing I can say. Nothing I *want* to say. I know I should give it up. Confess. Why should I keep pretending? My plan is ruined.

But as I look around the room at faces in front of me, something hard and angry starts to form itself inside my heart. First, I look at my mother, always the one in charge, so full of smothering, overwhelming concern; then at Mrs. T., regally self-righteous and accusing; at Valerie, sweetly confused; at Phil, vaguely embarrassed. Then, there's Gavin. What is he, exactly? I glance down at the paper he'd pressed into my hand.

> Meet me in the empty apartment. I just
> want to help. Trust me, okay????

Trust him? Can I? I glance around the room for him. He's by the back stairs. His eyes find mine.

He's not mocking me. He's for real. I finally see it, and I know he reads it in my face. He turns and vanishes.

I stand up and face Mrs. Thackeray.

"You can't prove anything," I say. My words come out perfectly clear. They're sharp, like bits of broken glass. Everyone understands. A little thrill runs through me.

Mrs. Thackeray's eyebrows almost disappear into her white hair.

"I beg your pardon?" she asks. Her voice ends in a surprised squeak.

Once again, everyone starts talking at the same time. Mom gets up and heads in my direction, but Zander holds onto her arm. She whirls back to him, annoyed, and says something that sounds angry. Phil leaves the shop. Valerie stares at me. When I meet her gaze she glances away. Sylvie has tears in her eyes. So does Ansel. Émile whispers to him, his head bent down to his son. His face is strained. Mrs. Thackeray stares at me. Her face is hard. I stare back. My legs shake. I'm terrified, but I won't let her win.

"We should go," Valerie says, shouting to be heard. "Thanks for inviting us, but . . ." her voice trails off and her face flushes pink when she realizes nobody is paying her any attention. Phil rushes back inside, shoving his way through the shell curtain.

"Where's Gavin?" he asks, his face crinkled with worry. "He isn't here."

"Allow me to say something," Mrs. Thackeray calls. She raises a hand, and the talk dies down.

"I've had the empty flat sprayed for rodents. Rosemary should not enter it for a few days," she says.

"But she told you she didn't . . ." Émile splutters. "This is crazy," he adds, looking at the ceiling. The old lady and I continue our staring contest, but when Phil speaks his words spark a sudden feeling of dread inside me.

"I think that's why Gavin coughed so much when we got here," he says. He darts his eyes around, still looking for his son. "He has asthma. I'm afraid the chemicals they used might bring on an attack. We should leave. He didn't bring his inhaler tonight."

"But where *is* he?" Valerie says.

And my dread turns to panic. I know where Gavin went. He went there, fully expecting me to follow. If something happens to him, it's my fault.

Twenty-Five

Once inside Marguerite's apartment the smell hits me immediately: it's overpowering, sharp but strangely sweet at the same time, making me gag. Is Gavin really in here? He can't be that stupid. I shout his name, but hear nothing. Maybe I'm wrong, but I have to be sure. If he's here, it's mostly my fault.

My eyes dart everywhere but find nothing. Then I hear a sound. A hoarse, rasping cough. I sprint to the kitchen and he's there, sitting on the floor. Lips blue, dark eyes wide, mouth open, gasping. As I reach for him, an iron grip circles my wrist and I'm jerked backward.

"I knew it was you, girl! Where is it?" Thomas bellows in my face.

"He can't breathe!" I scream. "He needs to get out of here!" My words are mangled.

"What?" Thomas says, taking a step back. He looks down at Gavin on the floor.

"Get up, you!" he screams. His face is a monster mask, contorted with rage. Gavin doesn't answer. He just sits there and tries to breathe. His coffee-colored eyes are round. He looks up at me with nothing in his expression but fear.

"Up!" Thomas screams. Still keeping his grip on me, he lunges toward Gavin, grabs his shoulder and shakes, hard. Gavin's head snaps back and forth.

"Stop it! He needs help!" I scream again. Thomas lets go of Gavin and shakes my own arm so hard I yell in pain.

"Where is it?" he roars. I stare helplessly as Gavin curls into a fetal position and gasps for breath.

"What?" I sob, feeling tears pour down my face. Gavin is going to die if we can't get out of here.

"Don't play innocent with me, girl!" Thomas screams. He lumbers over to me and jerks me by my arm, pulling me so close I smell sour sweat and pine tree aftershave. He leans his revolting face into mine, inches away. "It's time you learned your place! You've caused us enough trouble!" Still holding me by one arm, he lifts a bony fist into the air. "You tell me where it is, NOW!" he screams, as his arm starts to descend. I squeeze my eyes shut and turn my face to the side, fear curdling in my stomach. But Thomas's fist doesn't make contact. Instead, he bellows like a bull, clutches his head and lets me go. I fall to the floor and open my eyes.

I blink. Maybe the rodent-killing fog is giving me hallucinations. Mrs. Thackeray, tottering and tiny, has appeared in the kitchen, a look of shock and rage on her face. Still holding onto Marguerite's portrait when she came in, she saw what her sweet Tommy was up to and smacked him on the side of the head with the heavy wooden frame of the painting. I'd cheer if I weren't still so terrified.

Not to be deterred, Thomas snatches the portrait from his mother's hands, knocking it from her grasp. As it thumps onto the tiles, there's a sound of splintering wood and something small falls from the back of the frame and hits the floor with a metallic "ping." It's a tiny metal key. Thomas and I dive for it at the same time, and neon stars and galaxies explode in my eyes as our heads collide.

Sound detonates all around me as well. Booming voices bounce off the walls in Marguerite's home. Gentle, soft-spoken Émile, who never shouts, is screaming like a drill sergeant on steroids. He yells words I don't understand and I blink swirling supernovas out of my eyes in time to watch while Émile and Zander hustle Thomas outside. My mother shouts and sobs as her trembling hands cling to me. Phil and Valerie magically materialize, pull Gavin to his feet and rush him out, their pale faces terrified. Shouting and scuffling sounds fade away.

Mom finally stops yelling, helps me stand and leads me out of Marguerite's kitchen and through the ruined front room. She won't stop sniffling. My head pounds. I stumble over books and hear the crunch of something broken beneath my feet. We exit through the front door, which screeches as it opens, and totter down the stairs. Back in Sylvie's shop, I'm led to a chair at the long table. Mrs. Thackeray is already there, her ancient face now covered with confusion and fear.

Sylvie appears with an ice pack and I hold it to the bump that's forming on my head while I sit and stare at platters of congealing food. No one speaks. I hear the whir of Ansel's respirator. I wonder what he thinks about all this.

There's something small in my hand. I still have the little key that fell out of the portrait frame. I quickly close my fist over it and shove it into my back pocket along with the Wizards' key. Why do I feel the need to hide it? No one says anything. Maybe they don't notice in all the craziness.

Mom sits next to Mrs. Thackeray. She's crying again.

"Rosemary, I don't think I've ever been more disappointed. I want the truth, right now," she says in her weepiest voice. At those words, my throat is full of sand and my tongue turns to plastic inside my mouth, like it will never be able to form words again. I stare into Mom's red, puffy eyes. She always has this effect on me.

"We all want to hear what you have to say," Mrs. Thackeray murmurs. I look up, surprised. Across the table from me, she sits hunched over in her chair, hugging Marguerite's broken portrait to her scrawny chest, and she's somehow smaller. Even her voice is different. It's quiet and unsure.

"Well, Rosemary?" Mom says, snuffling. "What's going on? And tell the truth, this time!" she says, swiping away a tear. "You obviously *were* going into that apartment, weren't you, but you refused to admit it. No wonder that man was so angry! What did you do?" She continues to sob, softly, shoulders shaking.

I stare at a bowl of cold sauce that looks like lumpy vomit and I hate her. What did *I* do? Thomas was about to smash my face with his huge fist and it's *my* fault? I can't even look at her. So, I swallow, and look at Mrs. T. in front of me, who reminds me of a deflated balloon, crumpled and empty. My stomach twists for a second with my familiar worry that no words will come out right, but I know I have to speak.

"I didn't mean to steal from you," I tell her, wincing at how bad my words slur themselves together, like all the sounds are in such a rush that they trip all over each other as they leave my mouth.

"Ah. Well . . ." Mrs. T. begins to say, but her voice trails off. She seems at a loss for words. "But you did steal?" she asks, as if to confirm what she already knows. "All those paintings?"

My heart speeds up. "Yeah," I say. I hear Mom gasp, and hurry to add, "I didn't plan to." Words come out a little clearer this time. I'm trying hard, now, because I want her to understand. "I only went in to find the cat. I took the paintings because I thought *you* were stealing them. I didn't know you owned the place," I say, pausing to clear my throat. "I'll tell you where I hid the stuff. I kept going back to find letters, because I wanted to know about Marguerite's weak words," I add haltingly.

"Weak words?" Mrs. T. stammers, looking at me like I've sprouted an extra head.

"Yeah," I answer. "It says that in one of the letters." But Mrs. T. still looks blank. "Wait," I say, rising to my feet.

"Stop!" Mom barks. "You're not going anywhere,

young lady!"

"Mom," I plead. "Please!"

"I'd like to know what she means," a soft voice says from behind me, speaking English. We all turn to Ansel, who was watching and listening the whole time. "Please, let her go."

Mom shrugs, rolls her eyes, and motions for me to go. I run upstairs to my suitcase, still waiting beside Sylvie and Émile's front door. Returning with the ribbon-bound bundles of paper, I place them on the table in front of Mrs. Thackeray, who shoves dishes aside to make room. Everyone moves closer. I show them the first letter I read.

"Des mots faibles. Weak words."

"Ah," Mrs. Thackeray sighs.

"You understand?" I ask.

"Perhaps more than you might think," she says, looking up at me. Her beady eyes are watery. Before I can ask her what she means, Mrs. T. adds, "Did you find any jewelry, Rosemary?"

I look blankly at her.

Mrs. Thackeray tiredly rubs her eyes and continues. "My grandmother's jewels were supposed to be worth a fortune. We found a list of everything in her records." She holds Marguerite's portrait in front of her and gazes sadly at it. "We were convinced we'd find jewels worth millions, but we found nothing. Thomas was most upset. Times have been hard," she finishes, speaking in a near whisper.

"I didn't see any jewelry," I say. I flinch at how the word sounds, like a drunk slurring syllables together. Mrs. T. looks right into my eyes for a moment and nods.

"I believe you. I also believe, Rosemary, that you meant well when you took these paintings. I suppose you thought you were saving them."

"Saving them?" Mom blurts in an angry, incredulous voice. "Oh, I don't think so!"

She sniffs loudly and leans forward, glaring at me. I gape at her in shock. Her mouth is set into a thin line.

"Apparently my daughter Rosemary has decided to become a thief," she says through clenched teeth. "She stole a painting from her best friend's brother and used it to fool us all into thinking she had some artistic talent. Then, she stole another painting from someone here, likely from that apartment, and sent it to me in Idaho, claiming it was hers. Our little art thief apparently doesn't recognize the work of Gauguin."

"What?" Sylvie spluttered. Even Ansel exclaims out loud.

"No, Mom, I—"

"Enough! Go pack your things. We're leaving right now," Mom shouts. "The painting is at the Chicago Museum of Art, Mrs. Thackeray. I sent it to a friend who works there. It will be returned to you, unless you want to sell it. The head curator is drooling over it."

"Darla, maybe we should—" Sylvie starts to say in her halting English, but Mom cuts her off.

"No, Sylvie," Mom interrupts. "She's coming with me, this minute. I'm grateful to you for the kindness you've shown my daughter. I'm sorry that you've been repaid with lies and deception."

I stare at Mom's face, furious and pinched. It feels like

my life is draining away from my body. Then, someone puts a hand on my shoulder. The unexpected touch startles me, and suddenly, I'm flooded with emotions. It's as if I'm a cornered, wounded animal. They're all backing me into a cage, ready to take me back to captivity. I whirl and throw the hand off of me, screaming, "No!"

"Sorry," Zander murmurs. He backs up, holding his hand in the air, as if to show he means no harm. I hadn't noticed his return. I stare, breathing hard. Sylvie sees my face. She stands.

"No, Madame. She will not go with you," Sylvie says in a trembling voice.

"What?" Mom squeals. "Who do you think you are?"

"Can't you see what is happening? It already happened once, long ago, to a helpless child. I understood when I saw how frightened Rosie was of Thomas, and when I saw the painting of Rosie as a child. You think you have found someone you can trust, but you see how afraid your daughter was when Zander came into the room. Look at how she moves away from him! Don't you see it?"

"What are you saying?" Zander asks, his voice horrified. His face is drained of color. "I'd never, ever do anything to hurt Rosemary." He turns pleading eyes to Mom. "Darla?"

She doesn't answer right away. As the understanding of what Sylvie said dawns on her face, she hesitates, looking from Zander to me, with confusion covering her twisted features. Zander sees the doubt that clouds her mind. I read it in his face. It's breaking his heart. I hadn't planned to actually get him in trouble. He wasn't supposed to be here when I lied about him. But he is, and this is my only chance to get away from *her*. Slowly, shakily, I look at Sylvie and nod my head.

Mom gasps, puts her hand over her mouth, and stares at Zander, who shakes his head over and over in denial. He has tears in his eyes. Mom's eyes are wounded, betrayed, and furious.

My insides are coated with ice. *What have I done?*

If I keep quiet, I can stay here. Sylvie said so. I can be free.

A low rumbling sound fills the otherwise silent room. Fat Cat has entered the shop, and is rubbing his considerable bulk against my ankles. I plop down and scoop him into my lap, hugging him to me. I love him. I love Sylvie, and Émile, and my freedom. But I hate the lying. And I never wanted to hurt anyone. Not Zander. Not like this. No one deserves that.

Taking a deep breath, I speak, looking up at my mother. "Zander never did anything to me," my voice cracks.

Mom puts her hands over her face. Zander's body slumps as all the tension leaves him, and he closes his eyes.

"Why didn't you say that right away?" Mom asks in a hoarse voice, still keeping her hands over her eyes. "Rosemary, how could you?"

I can't speak. Not a single sound. The confusion of colors in Sylvie's bright shop whirls around in front of my eyes. It almost hurts to look. Mom breathes, in, out, in, out, faster and faster, and I know her impatience is growing. So is her anger.

She uncovers her eyes and marches to stand in front of me, towering over me and Fat Cat. He leaps from my lap and streaks from the room.

"Rosemary!" she hisses. It's a command, the way she speaks my name. The sounds are soft, but somehow sharp, like blades that were made to cut. Something in her dark eyes reminds me of the hardness I saw earlier in Thomas's face, when he shouted and threatened me, raising his fist. I feel something boiling inside the way it did earlier, when I stood up to Mrs. T. My frozen insides start to thaw. I gulp air, leap to my feet and shove my mother. She falls onto the floor and looks up at me with her eyes wide.

"You lock me in my room every night! Every single night!" I scream.

Zander gasps. "Darla?" he says.

"You never leave me alone, Mom!" I scream. "I can't get away! You're everywhere! You choose my clothes and you do my hair like I'm a baby! You always work at my schools! YOU NEVER LEAVE ME ALONE!"

The words I scream explode in the air around me, so that the entire room is filled with my rage.

"Rosemary?" Mom gasps. The sharpness is gone from her voice.

Did I do that? I stare in horror at the woman on the floor in front of me. I pushed my own mother down and screamed at her. Why? I feel myself melting inside, wanting to flee again. To hide. But I also want to explain. I want her to understand.

I want everyone to understand. But when I open my mouth to speak, nothing comes out right.

I bolt up the back stairs, into Sylvie's kitchen, and grab my painting. The still-wet paint leaves dark smudges on my fingers. I bring it back down to the shop, where Mom is still on the floor. I hold the painting in front of her face. As something dawns in her eyes, I understand what Sylvie meant when she said that when you create a work of art, you're saying something to the world.

Slowly, as if she's in a trance, Mom reaches out with a shaking finger to touch my painting. She whispers something, too soft to understand. She takes in a sudden, sharp breath of air.

Then, she speaks, her eyes never leaving my painting.

"So little," she whispers. "You were so little. My baby." She draws in a ragged breath. "I lost you in the big store. One minute you were with me, and then, you were gone." Tears pour from her eyes. Her voice shakes. "The people in the store, they looked for you, we kept calling your name, but you didn't answer. They called the police, but you were gone, my baby was gone . . ."

Mom presses her hands over her face, and then her whole body folds in on itself. Zander kneels beside her and wraps his arms around her, holding her while she sobs.

Someone sniffs. I turn to see who it is. It's Ansel, watching me with tears in his eyes. And suddenly, this time when I open my mouth, the words are all there; ready to spill from my lips, and once I start, it's like a dam breaks, and I know there's nothing I could do to stop this rushing wall of words.

Looking into Ansel's dark eyes, I speak to everyone. Sylvie, Émile, Ansel, Mom, Zander, and Mrs. Thackeray. I tell how my first taste of freedom felt. How I found Sylvie and Émile and chose them to be my new family. Why I thought there might be a permanent place for me here and how I didn't understand what happened to Ansel. I even tell them about Jada and the horrible things I said to her. I tell how my dream of being "normal" in France came to a crash that day I couldn't even order a sandwich, but I still didn't want to leave. It was better than being home.

My words become more and more tangled, but I keep talking. I talk about lightning on the wall, paintings and letters. I tell about Thomas and what happened the day I cut off my hair. I describe how I found Marguerite's portrait.

And suddenly, I'm done.

I collapse into the nearest chair and close my eyes. I am empty. Now, *I'm* the crumpled balloon.

Zander breaks the silence.

"You lock her in her room, Darla?" he says, in a voice so soft I barely catch the words. "Literally lock her in, so she can't get out?"

I open my eyes. Zan and Mom are still sitting on the floor, no longer embracing. Their eyes are searching, traveling over one another's crumpled forms, seeing things they never have before. Mom's tears have stopped but her face is a mascara-smeared wreck. She hugs herself.

"I do it to keep her safe, Zander," she says in a trembling voice. "To keep her *safe*," she wails, her voice echoing through the shop. "I couldn't stand the thought of ever losing her again!"

Zander catches my eye. I try to smile but can't. His

lips twitch for a second or two. He's doing exactly what I'm doing; trying to make his face look like he's okay when he's ripped up inside. But that would take both of us way more than we've got, so we drop the facade and just stare at each other.

I cannot believe what I was about to do to him. My voice has gone into hiding, so I mouth the words instead.

I'm sorry.

Zander's face is still. His eyes are pools of sorrow. Then, his lips press together and curve upward, forming a tiny smile.

"I saw my entire life flash before me, kid," he says in a hoarse voice. "Thank you for telling the truth."

He turns back to Mom.

"I helped Rosemary do this, Darla," he says. He rolls his eyes. "Well, not *this*," he says, making a sweeping gesture with his arm to indicate the shop around us. "I wasn't aware she was going to travel to Nice, but I helped her get to France because I felt like she needed to be on her own for a while. To gain more confidence. To believe in herself. Frankly, I think it worked." He scoots closer to Mom. She doesn't look at him. "Don't you think so, Darla?" Zander adds in a whisper.

Mom doesn't say anything. She keeps her head down. Tears fall onto fists clenched tight in her lap.

I put my face in my hands. She doesn't get it. What if she never does?

At first, I hear nothing but the soft whir of the machine that breathes for Ansel, but then, there's a shuffling sound. I open my eyes. Mom is crawling across the floor. She reaches me and takes my hand. I start to pull away, but freeze when I see her face. Something is different. The hardness is gone. So is the anger.

"Rosemary," she whispers. "I'm the one who should apologize. I am truly, truly sorry. Please forgive me."

Twenty-Six

It's a miracle that I'm here, inside Marguerite's apartment. It's a miracle that Mom and Zander went to a hotel last night and left me here, with Sylvie and Émile. But they're coming for me later. I don't have much time.

The wardrobe doors lurch open with a small screech. Her dresses have been hung up again. The carnation silk waves gently at me, like an old friend welcoming me back. I smell the same, faint perfume I'd noticed before, but now something sparks a memory and I recognize it. It's the scent from the bottle I found in here and threw against the wall.

Gently pushing the dresses aside, I shine my flashlight onto the back of the wardrobe. As I thought, there's a tiny door. The silver key from the frame of Marguerite's portrait fits perfectly into the keyhole. The key turns easily and the door pops open. Behind it is a square compartment, with barely enough room for the bundle of letters hiding there. They're tied with a faded ribbon that must have once been blood-red.

Cara mia, the letter begins. Great. Spanish? Italian? I can't read these! Disappointment pricks at me. But I leaf through them, fingering the faded letters, slanted and curling, so pretty as they move across the pages in lacy patterns. The papers make dry, rustling sounds as I turn them, and a faint whiff of wood smoke tinged with something sweet wafts to my nose.

Bundling the brittle papers back together, I turn to go. I shouldn't be in here. I only wanted to try the key. And say goodbye.

Hardly breathing, I tiptoe through the ruined rooms. The chemical smell has cleared away. I don't know who opened the windows and left them gaping wide, but I'm grateful. The apartment is quiet. Faint noises, mere whispers of sound filter into Marguerite's home from outside. The soft whoosh of early-morning traffic, clatters and thuds as workers load garbage into a battered truck, the whir of the first tram whizzing by, all are muted and far-away sounding. Marguerite's home is from another time, another century. It's as if the modern world doesn't dare intrude. Maybe that's why I like it so much.

Turning for one last look, I say goodbye to peeling wallpaper, faded curtains, massive chandeliers and wooden-beamed ceilings. What will happen to this place? Will Mrs. T. still let her son destroy it? I hope not, but it's not my concern. It never was. Right now, I'm mostly worried about what will happen to me. I don't have long to wait. Mom and Zander said they'd sleep late, but they'll be here as soon as they wake up.

And then, as I shuffle back to Ansel's bedroom, through the dark, cramped passage, I drop the letters. The ribbon breaks and the pages scatter in a heap at my feet on the dusty floorboards. When I bend down to gather them together, my flashlight illuminates one of the papers. It's a sketch of Marguerite, a black and white version of the portrait I'd found of her inside the wardrobe, with a name scrawled across the bottom corner.

Something tells me this is important. I want to show Sylvie, but she and Émile are still asleep. Their coffeepot clock ticks softly, the only noise in the sleepy apartment. I'll go to Mrs. Thackeray, since I need to return this key and the letters anyway, but when I creep up the stairs and knock at her door, no one answers.

Ansel. His name, his face rushes to my mind. The moment I think it, I know I have to talk to him. I never apologized for the things I said to him. This is likely my only chance.

I take the tram that heads up the big hill, because his hospital's at the top. I hop off before it gets too close, though. Now that I'm here, doubts flood my heart. What if he refuses to see me? How will I say what I need to say? Will he understand me?

Go on, stupid. You owe him. I keep walking.

The smelly hallway is quiet. Most doors are closed and I start to relax, thinking I won't be able to visit Ansel. As I creep along I list excuses in my head: *it's too early. I tried, but he was asleep. It wasn't my fault.* And then, when I reach Ansel's room, the painted beach door is wide open.

I peer around the doorframe. He's awake. He sits in his chair, intently staring at a laptop on the table in front of him. The screen is a whirl of colors. It displays what looks like the painting of a young woman walking along the beach. She holds a stick in one hand and writes letters in the wet sand. The girl has short, dark hair. As I watch, something on the screen moves. Smears of lighter brown and gold appear on the girl's dark head, making it look as if the bright sun is shining down on her hair. Then, I read the letters the girl has written in the sand. Écoutez-moi. Listen to me.

"That's me!" I whisper.

Ansel isn't at all surprised to see me. He smiles and asks me to come in. Then, he places his lips on the little control I'd seen before, the one I saw him use to move his wheelchair, and again more colors are added to the image on the screen. He's painting with a computer.

I watch for a few minutes, while Ansel adds a brush stroke here or there, erases it, and tries again. He never seems satisfied with the result. Finally, he sighs and lifts his head.

"Do you like it?" he asks.

"Yes," I answer. "I never knew you could . . ." my words trail off and bite the dust. I don't think he understands me, because he doesn't answer. Instead, he uses his control to click on the corner of the screen and the painting disappears. "Could you pull that cord, there by the bed? I need to call the nurse."

After I do, I'm completely at a loss for words. Ansel watches me, his face thoughtful, unsmiling. I can't figure out how to say what I want to, and I'm sure it won't sound right, anyway. I give up and pull the letters from my bag.

"Look," I say, as I place the drawing on the table.

"The portrait of Marguerite," Ansel says. He stares for a moment, as if he too is at a loss for words. Then he looks up at me with a gleam of laughter in his eyes. "Rosie, did you read the signature?"

"Yeah," I say, shrugging. I'm not about to try to say the name. I still hear Gavin's voice in my head as he mocks me for slaughtering that word.

"Antonio Grimaldi," Ansel says, speaking in an incredulous tone. "You don't know who he is?"

I'm tired of talking. I shrug.

Ansel laughs. "Rosie, you must learn your art history," he says, chuckling. "Who is he? A very famous Italian artist!" He pauses to catch his breath. "I remember reading once that he was in love with a French actress. And to think, it was Marguerite! *Our* Marguerite, who lived right next door! *Fantastique*!"

I like how he says "our" Marguerite. We smile to each other for a moment. Then Ansel looks at his laptop.

"It's true I am still able to paint in this way," he murmurs. "But it's not the same." He turns to look back at me, his dark eyes holding mine. "When I first woke up in the hospital and knew I could no longer use my hands, I wanted to die."

My eyes can't leave his.

"I've always had the power to form words with my mouth, but my hands were my true voice. Do you understand?" he asks.

I nod, slowly, finally ready to speak.

"Ansel, I didn't want to hurt you. I was upset. I'm sorry," I say, slowly, haltingly, feeling the still-strange sounds of another language bounce around in my mouth, cursing my stupid tongue for never working right. At least the words are recognizable, if not perfect.

His beautiful smile spreads across his face. "I understand. Thank you."

We don't speak after that for a while, but for once, I don't mind the silence. I know Ansel doesn't, either. There aren't many people who understand that every single second of an interaction doesn't need to be filled with words. They're a rare breed, and I can tell that Ansel is one of them.

Ansel's screen saver goes on, and a series of photographs of Nice flash onto the screen. I smile at a picture of "the pole guys," as I've come to think of them. Giant night-lights.

"The Conversation," Ansel murmurs. He glances at me. "Did you know that's the name of this sculpture?"

"No," I say. "Why?"

"They speak at night when they light up. Each statue represents one of the seven continents, and when the colors change, it shows that they are talking to one other."

"*Sans mots*," I whisper. Without words.

"*Oui*," Ansel whispers. His eyes meet mine. I blink hard to force away tears.

The nurse, a gaunt woman with grey strands of hair pulled into a sparse bun and the haze of a mustache on her upper lip comes in. Her eyes size me up in an unfriendly way. Knowing I'm being dismissed, I pick up the drawing and get ready to leave.

"Rosie," Ansel says as I reach the door. "You and I have much in common. We both must find different ways to tell the world who we are. That's what I was trying to show with this painting. When I finish it, it will be yours."

Tears fill my eyes. This time I let them fall. I don't trust my voice, so I smile, nod, and fly away.

Twenty-Seven

The morning air is already warm. The briny scent of the ocean and the smell of wet plants and trees fills my nose. Colors fill my head as I watch the scenery blur by. I don't want to say goodbye to this place.

When I get off the tram at the stop closest to Sylvie's, someone walks toward me. Someone wearing neon purple board shorts, with orange flames on the sides. I'm glad he's okay, but that doesn't mean I want to see him.

But I should. He went into the apartment, thinking I was going to follow. And, he said he wanted to help me. How?

The dark smudges under Gavin's eyes stand out in stark contrast to his pale skin and fiery hair.

"Hey," he says, with a kind of half-hearted smile.

"Hey," I say back after a long second.

We stare at each other. He twitches and scratches at his ear. I look away and pick at my nails. *This is going well.*

Then Gavin blurts, "Can I talk to you?" He pulls out an inhaler and takes a couple of puffs.

"You okay?" I say, not wanting to answer his question.

"Yeah," he says. Putting the inhaler in his pocket, he looks at me with a tiny smile. "Can we walk for a while?" I'm not about to give in, but at that moment I happen to look farther down the street. The unmistakable figures of Mom and Zander exit their bright red rental car in front of Sylvie's building.

"Come on," I say, taking Gavin's arm and pulling him with me in the opposite direction. I'm not ready to give up my last moments of freedom. Not yet.

We pass shops opening up for the morning, men and women in business suits, hurrying down the sidewalk, a bald man sweeping his steps, a cigarette that's mostly ashes dangling from his mouth. A stray cat darts in front of us with a mouse dangling from its jaws.

"Hey, can I buy you breakfast?" Gavin blurts. I look up from the cat and dead mouse in surprise and laugh. Just a little.

"Sorry, I guess my timing was off," Gavin says with a wry grin. "But let's find someplace where we can eat." I shrug and Gavin takes it as a "yes," so we keep going, continuing to walk in what might almost be a companionable silence, except for the fact that I still don't want to say anything. I hate letting anyone hear how I talk. Lost in thought, streets blur by, but suddenly Gavin stops.

"What about this place?" he asks.

My eyes dart up and for the first time I realize where

I am. A vivid yellow banana-shaped sign screams its presence to the world. We've arrived at the one place I never planned to return to. And Gavin is already opening the door for me, waiting.

Inside it's cool and smells like fried food. As my eyes adjust to the dim light after being outside in the morning sun, I pray, *Please, please, please, don't let* him *be here.* I blink and look at the counter.

Of course, he's here. Andreas of the Gorgeous Eyes. The guy who ignored me and let me stand for an eternal fifteen minutes, pushed aside by the crowd, is standing behind the counter. No one else is around. It's our turn.

"Order something for me, okay?" Gavin says. I glance back at him. Order for him? Is he serious? He's taunting me. He's making fun of me, looking for any chance he can get to make me talk, because he knows I'll sound stupid. But then I notice the red streaks creeping up his pale cheeks, and I see the sheepish look in his eyes.

"You know I can't speak French," Gavin says.

The guy behind the counter clears his throat. I glance into his face. A flash of recognition glints in his eyes. He remembers me. I take a step back. I feel myself withering, shrinking, wanting to run. It's what I always do. But some day, I have to find my feet, and I have to make them stop walking away.

My mouth feels like it's filled with sand, like it always is when I have to speak to strangers. But I force myself to open my mouth and speak. The guy waits. I look at a spot above his face, try not to think about how cute he is, and say the words.

"*Deux croque-chocolate bananes.*" Then, I wilt inside. My words came out about as mushy as cooked bananas.

The young man says, "I'm sorry, mademoiselle, what did you say?" I look into his face. His forehead, like before, is crinkled. I can clearly read the look of annoyance in his eyes.

A tall blonde girl sidles up to the counter and smiles at Andreas and he grins back and moves away from me to stand in front of her. And like always, Rosemary turns into wallpaper.

A few more customers squeeze through tables and chairs and head up to the counter, and I find myself being pushed even farther aside. With a burning face I pull out my borrowed cell phone and type, *2 croque chocolat-bananes.* Then I shout, "*Pardon*!"

Heads swivel in my direction. I elbow my way back to the counter, in front of the cute guy. I look up into the amber eyes and shove the cell phone at his face, a little too close. He jerks his head back, but I stay where I am, holding the phone in front of his wide eyes. Finally, he looks at the screen, glances up at me, then back down at the screen. His lips move as he reads. Then, he smiles. His front teeth are large, and stick out a tiny bit. It takes the edge off the gorgeous factor for me.

Andreas reminds me of a ferret. I start to giggle.

The boy turns to make the sandwiches and I keep giggling. Everyone stares. Some eyes are friendly, some, including the blonde girl's, are not. What, she has a problem with *me*? Like mush-mouthed Rosemary is some kind of competition? I laugh harder and a couple of tears run down my face. Gavin gives my back a couple of weak pats, but soon drops his hand. I'm sure he thinks I've lost it.

The guy puts our sandwiches on the counter and Gavin pays, saying, "*Merci beaucoup,*" with the worst American accent possible, actually pronouncing the silent "p" at the end. The beautiful ferret-faced Andreas smiles at us in his rodent way. I grab our sandwiches, still laughing, and we go outside. Gavin takes the warm, fried chocolate-banana sandwich I hand him with a strange look.

"What was that all about?" Gavin asks me.

"Nothing," I say, still laughing. But it was everything. To me, anyway. I take a bite of my sandwich. It's even better than I remembered.

"Dang. These are good," Gavin says around a mouthful of gooey bananas and melted chocolate.

"Mm-hmm," I say. We eat on a park bench and watch the world go by. And eventually, we finish our food and have to start talking.

"Thanks for ordering for me," Gavin says. "And, thanks for, well, you know, for kind of saving my life, even though . . ." His voice trails off. More red blotches creep up over his face.

"Even though what?" I say, admittedly enjoying his discomfort.

"Thanks for saving my life, even though I was kind of a jerk."

He gets that? I have to ask him about it.

"Why?" I say, looking into his face.

"Why what?" Gavin asks me back. His eyes are wide

open. He really doesn't know what I'm asking? I sigh. Everybody always wants me to say more.

"Why did you make fun of me that first day?" I ask, slowly, inwardly cringing at the sounds and syllables that trip over themselves.

"I guess I didn't really know how to talk to you," Gavin says. He pauses to wad up the paper from his sandwich and tosses it into a nearby garbage can. "I didn't want to come here in the first place with my Dad and his new wife. He left my Mom for her, you know that?" he says, his eyes glittering with anger.

Oh. All the times Gavin called her *Valerie.* Not Mom. His voice took on a razor's edge whenever he spoke of her. And I was too wrapped up in my own stupid problems to see what was right in front of me.

"I'm sorry," I whisper.

"I know," Gavin says. "Anyway, this trip is . . . well, it's their *honeymoon*," he adds with a cringe. "But Dad insisted that I come so they dragged me along with them, and it was as miserable as I imagined. Then, one day something good happened. We went into a souvenir shop and this hot girl was there, smiling me."

Hot girl? I feel a pleasant sensation somewhere in the pit of my stomach.

"So I went to talk to her," Gavin says, "but when she said her name, it came out a little weird. I guess I reacted without thinking. I so did not expect something like that. I thought for a second that you did it on purpose." He cringes. "Stupid, I know! I should never have made fun of you."

"No." I say simply. But I can't help smiling a little as I say it.

"You did stuff, too, you know. You dumped your drink on my lap, and you made fun of me when I couldn't speak French, but I kind of figured I deserved it, after the way I treated you. I really tried to get to know you, Rosemary. I wanted to let you know that it doesn't matter how you talk."

He reads my incredulous expression and hurries on.

"I'm serious! I've never met someone like you before, and I didn't really know how to talk to you. So, I'm sorry. Again. I'm sorry for being a jerk. And yesterday when that old lady accused you of taking her stuff, I figured that I owed it to you to help. I was going to pretend that I was the one taking stuff from that apartment."

There's so much I want to say right now. But there's something else I want to do more. So I do.

Gavin kisses me back. Chocolate and bananas taste way better than bubblegum.

Then we talk for a while. Not about anything important. And we don't talk a lot, either. I'm still not used to having anyone hear how tangled my words are, other than Jada, Mom, and Zander.

A church bell tolls. It's late, so I stand up. I still don't know what to do with my hands, so I shove them in my pockets.

"You're probably gonna be going home, aren't you?" Gavin asks, rising to walk with me back to Sylvie's shop.

"Yeah." It hurts to say it.

"Will you keep in touch?" he asks. He reaches out for

my hand so I let him take it. And then I'm holding hands with a boy for the first time in my life . . . It's weirdly wonderful and confusing all at the same time.

I nod, not trusting my voice. Gavin writes his number on a gum wrapper and gives it to me.

"I gotta go," he finally says.

I want to kiss him again but by now we're in front of the shop. I can't see anyone inside but I feel someone, somewhere, staring.

Gavin gets it. He kisses me on the cheek. I watch him while he walks away until he's lost in a swarm of buzzing tourists.

A breeze blows through my short hair, bringing with it the scent of the ocean. I close my eyes and pretend that the currents of cool air are pulling some thoughts out of my brain, scattering them over the Mediterranean, making me forget. And putting other thoughts back inside.

I have to learn to do that. I have to forget about some things. How it feels when someone doesn't understand me. What it's like when someone makes fun of me. I have to get over it!

Because there are people like Gavin. People who will be patient enough to get to know me. And understand me.

Anyway, like Ansel says, I can find different ways of saying what I want to say.

I turn to go inside, ready to face whatever is waiting for me.

Twenty-Eight

The waiting area in the airport smells like expensive perfume. We're right outside a gift shop. From somewhere inside it, I'd swear I heard the sound of breaking glass. It makes me smile.

Mom and I don't talk much while we wait. I check out my new phone, and my smile fades.

I have six numbers in my contacts list, now. Gavin. Mom and Zander. Sylvie. Nicole (who finally remembered who I was yesterday). Jada.

I've heard nothing from her since I said those horrible words. I've called, emailed, texted, tried Twitter. Jada's silence sticks in my gut and twists itself when I lay awake at night, thinking about it. I know some things aren't easy to fix. And I'm so afraid this never will be.

Mom has the small painting I made for Jada inside her carry-on bag. I didn't really do it all myself. Ansel coached me a lot. I have no idea what Jada might think of it. If, that is, she chooses to accept it. It shows Jada and Mitch, together holding hands. They face one another as they get married. Mom hates it. I guess the part she doesn't like is that Jada and Mitch are both standing up. No wheelchairs in sight. I think Jada will totally be into it, though, if . . .

If she ever sees it.

I have to try one more time. I take out the painting, prop it up against my chair and take a photo of it. I email it to Jada while Mom carefully re-wraps the small canvas and puts it back in her bag.

"Are you sure about this?" Mom asks in a tiny voice. It's the same thing she's asked for the past three weeks.

"Yes," I answer. I'm scared. But I'm sure.

Mom's eyes fill with tears. "It's only until Christmas," she reminds me.

"I know," I say.

I'm doing a semester abroad. Some classes at my new school in Nice will be in English. Some will be in French. Crazy? Probably. Anyway, I'll be with other American students studying French. We'll all slaughter the language together. And in December, I'll go back to Twin Falls for the rest of the school year. It will be different. Mom quit her job at my school. I'll be there solo for the first time in my life.

And she promised to remove the lock from the outside of my bedroom door. No more schedule. No Matching Shirt Mondays. I choose my clothes. And my friends. Who knows? Maybe I'll even start dating. Eventually.

Whenever I think about my plan, I cringe a little on the inside. I was so desperate to escape that I didn't get how insane it really was.

I'm invited to return to France next summer. Every summer after that, if I want. After all, I'm an artist. At least, I think I am. The lie is becoming something less than a lie, although not yet quite true. Maybe it's a half-lie? Ansel keeps saying that I was telling the truth because I have an artist's eyes. Whatever that means.

Mom looks down at her new diamond ring and her eyes fill with even more tears. Zander hands Mom a tissue.

"Change is good," he says with a smile. I can't believe what happened. He still wants to marry Mom after everything. After the crazy stuff he found out about my mother, like her total over-protective insanity. After what I almost did to him. He believes in Mom, and he forgave me. Anyway, his eyebrow ring isn't that bad. I'll have to get used to it at any rate.

My phone beeps and my heart stops.

Girlfriend. You there?

My fingers barely work. I text as fast as I can.

J! I'm soooo, so sorry! I didn't mean it! I love you. Please forgive me. Please!!!!!

I type so fast I spell everything wrong. But Jada always understands me.

I don't breathe while I wait. Ten seconds. Fifteen. Twenty-two.

I like the picture. Beautiful. We'll talk later. Miss you.

My eyes fill with tears. You can't ever take back the horrible things you say. They're always there, hanging in the air between you and the one who was hurt by them. All you can do is hope you will be forgiven. After so many weeks of Jada's silence, I'd almost stopped hoping.

Sylvie and Émile arrive right as Mom and Zander's plane is announced. Mom clings to me and I feel her heart pounding. But Zander gently peels her off and I tell her that I love her. That I promise I'll text and email. Every day. That I'll stay out of trouble. This time.

And she lets me go.

Palm trees welcome me with gentle waves as we drive by. Warm air flows in through the windows. Sylvie hums softly to herself. Émile points out things as we pass: the old fort, the Promenade des Anglais, rows of blue umbrellas on the beach. As if I haven't seen them before. And every so often, he repeats a number to himself, shaking his head in disbelief. "Two and a half million," he says, with a funny expression. That's how much someone paid for Marguerite's portrait at an auction. Mrs. Thackeray is still haggling with the art museum over the Gauguin. It's supposed to be worth even more.

Émile and Sylvie smile at each other often. I guess the money Mrs. Thackeray got from selling Marguerite's painting made her feel generous about the apartments and she didn't adjust anyone's rent. She also didn't hand everything over to her son. He'd have a hard time taking care of it all from prison, anyway. Mrs. T. confided in Sylvie, who confided in me. Apparently her son has anger management issues. Thomas had served some time in England for assault but was on parole. He missed checking in with his "offender manager" while he was busy looking for lost jewels and bullying me. So, he's back behind bars in England. Jolly good.

Well, the best news of all is that the building is going co-op. After having lived there for so long, Sylvie and Émile will only have to pay a few more years before they own their apartment and the shop.

The studio behind the shop is in disarray. Workers are pounding hammers, painting and even installing a bathroom, complete with a special tub that has a door on the side. Everything is for Ansel. "We can all paint together," Sylvie says with a twinkling smile.

Soon I'm back in my borrowed bedroom. My bedroom. The hole in the wall is sealed. The door is painted shut. Ansel's ocean is angry and dark, but I notice for the first time that there's a glimmer up high near the ceiling, where painted stars peek out from behind the gloom. A bare patch catches my attention. I wonder if Ansel ever planned to fill it in. I hope he won't mind if I do.

I form the Milky Way in miniature high up on the wall with tiny gold and white dots of paint. Finished, I lie down on the bed to admire my work. It's not bad. Maybe I *do* have an artist's eyes. At least I have my own, unique way of seeing the world. I trace the lines on my palm and remember the day, not long ago, when I broke the bottle and cut myself. In my mind, the sparkling grains of sand swirl like a glittering galaxy on my skin.

Tomorrow I go to a new school in a foreign country where they speak a different language. I can't even speak my own language that well. I told Mom I was sure this was what I wanted, but . . . is it, really?

My insides quiver. I squeeze my eyes shut and hug myself to keep from shaking. I hate what it's like when I meet new people. I hate the confused looks. I hate the mockery. And most of all I hate the pity. But Marguerite didn't let any of that stop her. Google told me.

I smile at my galaxy. Marguerite acted all her life; until her death at the age of ninety-three. She moved to America and kept working. She was even in one of the first "talkies," or movies with sound. I watched it on YouTube.

Nothing stopped her. I won't let anything stop me.

And I finally understand something. Maybe what matters the most isn't *how* I say anything. What truly matters is *what* I say.

The painted galaxy glitters above me. Fat Cat purrs at my feet.

I'm still scared. Maybe I always will be, at least a little, but I won't back down. I can bring it. After all, I once held a tiny piece of the universe in the palm of my hand.